Hardships and Blessings Growing Up on Chicago's Westside

A Novel

By

Wayne L. Meyer

and

Meryl L. Wilens

Acknowledgements

In memory of Mom and Dad and my second Mom, Ruth Inendino.

Thank you for being there when I needed you most. You have left me with great memories which I cherish.

WLM

For my mother who gathered friends to play Mah Jongg each week, giving them time to share their stories. They spoke of sorrows and ailments never taken seriously by their families or their doctors. They told of treatments that did more harm than good. Together, they offered hope to each other and enriched my understanding of women's lives.

MLW

CHAPTER ONE

Sometimes you know your life has changed at the very moment it happens. Such as when you say "I do" at the altar. Or when you hold your baby for the first time. Other times, it is only when you look back that you know, "That was when my life took a totally new direction."

For me, it happened in 1959, on a very hot July afternoon in the Columbus Park neighborhood on Chicago's Westside. I was eleven when I walked across a parking lot and everything in my life began to change.

Back then, the Columbus Park neighborhood in Chicago was not a bad place to be a kid. The world did not intrude every minute of every day, like it does today. I knew there was a big world out there but my life focused on the families and kids who lived a few blocks around me.

In the fifties, what our families called "our neighborhood" was where people like us lived— immigrants or children of immigrants from the same part of the world, eating the same foods and celebrating the same holidays. One or two blocks over, it could seem very foreign—names were harder to pronounce, odors wafting from kitchens were different and houses were decorated for different holidays. Crossing from one street to the

1

next could be as fraught with anxiety as crossing the divide between East and West Berlin, if you remember the time before Berlin was again one city as it is today.

Most of the kids in my neighborhood had American parents but their grandparents had come to the States from someplace in Europe. I remember being surprised that my buddy, Johnny Williamson, had grandparents who spoke perfect English. His family had come over before the Civil War. All the other grandparents I knew had accents. When I was real young, I believed that to be a grandparent, you had to have come over from "the old country" and speak with an accent. And be short.

My block was the border between two parts of Columbus Park. Our block was still very Jewish. On one end, there was Rosen's Appetizing. Our mothers called it "Tiffany's" because of the high cost of the food they sold. At the other end of the block was the synagogue we didn't go to. My dad had argued with people there over how much they charged for Hebrew school so I had to walk all the way to B'nai Israel of Austin Park for Jewish classes.

Right behind that synagogue, facing the other block but sharing the same parking lot, was a big church. We Jewish kids just called it The Church. The Catholic kids called it Christ the King.

A stranger coming to the area might not notice any differences between the two blocks. After all, the houses on that block looked just like the houses on our block.

We kids knew the difference. Once you crossed the parking lot to the street the Church faced, the kids were mostly Italian with some Irish mixed in. We didn't go there often.

Our neighborhood was called Columbus Park because "The Park" was just a few blocks away. It was a dream world for a city kid. It had a lagoon where you could rent a boat to go fishing. It had baseball fields, a nine-hole golf course, a pool and lots of open space.

That summer of 1959 was the first time I could go to The Park without "adult supervision." Dad had finally given in because I was sneaking into The Park on my own anyway to escape from home because of the "situation" there. Whenever Dad found out, he whipped me with his belt. He said it was for my own good, to keep me safe, but it only made me want to stay away from home more. So that summer, he decided, that rather than having to keep whipping me for roaming the streets alone, he would let me go to the Park with friends he approved of. Mostly that was my cousin Sam.

If I stayed in our neighborhood, Sam, our friends and I played Pinners, a ball game played against the stoops of buildings. We fought over every point. Most often I played Pinners on Sam's block, where life was better for me.

Sam's parents were my Aunt Jennie, my father's sister, and her husband, Uncle Bernie Gordon. Sam was three years older than me and his sister, Sherrie, was five years older. Sam and Sherrie understood why my older sister Karen and I wanted to stay away from home, away from our mother's confusion and the fighting between our parents that made the air in our apartment heavy with tension. We also wanted to be far from Dad's anger and his belt.

It was very hot that day in July, as hot as an iron skillet. Moisture hung heavy in the still air in our neighborhood, far from Lake Michigan's cooling breezes.

When we saw waves of heat rising from the street, we couldn't bear to play anything. We were too old to run in and out of the water from the hydrants in our underwear as we did as little kids so we found cooler alternatives. We usually wandered over to Madison Street.

Like The Park, Madison Street had lots of great places. Along with the movie theatre, there was the

Cinderella Bowling Alley and our favorite, Finkelman's Drugstore.

We loved Finkelman's because it was air-conditioned, not just air-cooled. It had racks of comic books and magazines that we would read, pretending that we were deciding which to buy but just trying to finish the story. There were packets of Topps baseball cards with a flat rectangle of bright pink chewing gum that was just in the way when you were desperate to know if you had gotten Sandy Koufax, Mickey Mantle, Hank Aaron or Ernie Banks.

Old man Finkelman was nice. His only kid, Arnold, had been killed in WWII. He never chased us out even when he knew we didn't have money to buy anything. He asked us about our favorite teams and listened to what we had to say.

Sometimes we had money from returning soda bottles collected from neighbors' trash and getting the nickel or two cents deposit on each one. We would then sit at the counter like real customers.

My favorite drink was a chocolate phosphate. I loved watching Finkelman make it. He pressed the syrup bottle two quick times then he added seltzer from the hose with the nozzle. He pretended not to watch, but always stopped just as the seltzer reached the top of the glass.

On this day, all the boys in our gang gave up playing Pinners after just a few innings. It was too hot, they said. Besides, it was lunchtime so boys headed home.

There was no one calling Sam and me home for lunch. My mother was so confused about time, she never knew when it was lunchtime. Sam's mother, Aunt Jennie, wasn't home because she worked at the Veriflex factory, assembling file folder holders. Dad had worked there for years and had helped her get the job.

Dad was an important man at Veriflex. He was a genius at repairing the factory's equipment. He complained all the time that he wasn't being paid enough for keeping all the machines running. Without him, he said, there would be no Veriflex folder holders going out the door.

Sam's mom, Aunt Jennie, always made him a bag lunch before she left for work. His lunch had two of everything, two peanut butter and jelly sandwiches, two apples, and two cartons of juice.

It wasn't that Sam was such a big eater. It was just that Aunt Jennie knew "our situation." Each day, Sam shared his lunch with me and his sister Sherrie shared her lunch with my sister Karen. I didn't know it then but Dad slipped Aunt Jennie a few bucks each week for those lunches.

"Our situation" was the polite phrase for the chaos caused by my mother. At eleven, I didn't know the name for my mother's problem but I knew that she was often not in the same world as my dad, Karen and me. Some days, she was there with us; other days, she was marooned on a distant island in her mind.

On those island days, she would set off to do something but end up doing something totally different. She would go shopping for groceries, only to come home hours later with nothing. Or she gave us a crinkled brown bag like it was a great present.

"Open it," she would urge us, her brown eyes wide. "I picked it out just for you."

We had learned to play along with her moods, so, as Karen slowly unrolled the top of the bag, she tried to look thrilled at what was inside.

One day, she pulled out a paper doll book, something she liked when she was eight years old but not now that she was thirteen. I pulled out a set of jacks and a small ball, a little girl's toy.

We knew there was no point in reminding Mom that I was an eleven-year-old boy and Karen was a teenager. If we didn't act happy, she would run into the bedroom, lock the door and stay there until Dad got home. Then he would yell at us for making her cry and at Mom for making a scene.

Those were the days we had no lunch because there was no food in the house. Other days, we made our own lunches from what we found. We ate many cucumber and onion sandwiches. That is why we were always glad to visit our cousins, so we could picnic out of the bag lunches Aunt Jennie had made for her kids. And for us.

That July day, Sam plucked his sandwich out of the bag then handed it to me. He never made me feel bad about not being able to share back. Sam was good that way. He understood my situation.

And I understood his. Sam and his sister Sherrie both had had polio. As our Zayde said, "That family ain't got no *mazel!*" No luck with two kids struck with the same disease.

The first vaccine against polio, the Salk vaccine, was available only since 1954. Each summer, for decades before that, fear of polio closed parks and pools and theatres, anywhere crowds gathered. People who could afford it left the city for a summer in the country where mothers and kids stayed all week, fathers coming for the weekends. Other families, like ours, stayed put and took their chances.

My cousins were two of the unfortunates left marked by the disease. Sherrie had one foot shorter than the other and wore ugly shoes, one having a very thick sole to make her stand and walk evenly. Sam had to wear a brace on one leg. He limped, but he never complained. He never asked for extra treatment when we played Pinners. He just did the best he could.

I never mentioned his limp. It was just what he had to deal with, just like my sharing lunch out of his bag was the way I got a good meal.

On that day, as we ate, Sam exclaimed, "Jeez, it's hot. How about heading over to Finkelman's? We can cool off there. That'd be good. Let's go."

That was Sam's way. He shared everything with me, even a plan he came up with himself. He made it sound like we had discussed it and agreed on it. His ideas were usually good but soon I was not so sure about this one.

Right then, I nodded as I finished my apple and tossed the core to the curb. I folded over the mouth of the empty paper bag, held it almost closed then blew into it. I smacked it to make it explode. It was my daily ritual.

I tossed the scraps of brown paper into the trash can and waited for Sam to stand up, never an easy task with the heavy brace on his leg. I turned right to go the long way around the block towards Finkelman's.

Sam shook his head, turning in the opposite direction. "It's too hot to go the long way around. Let's cut across 'the lot' and go down Gladys. Yeah, that's what we'll do. We'll go the short way down Gladys."

I hesitated. Gladys Street was the street The Church faced. It was not *our* neighborhood. On Gladys, the houses had statues of sad-eyed ladies in flowing blue robes. Zucchini vines and tomato plants grew in every tiny bit of soil. The women sitting at the windows spoke loudly across the alleys in Italian. And the kids… Well, there were more of them and they seemed rougher and tougher than the kids on our block.

But Sam had already set off. Despite his limp and his leg brace, I had to rush to catch up.

"I don't know if this is a good idea, Sam," I muttered as we crossed The Church's lot and started down Gladys. When I saw the boys down the block, I knew it was a very bad idea.

I don't know what they were doing before they spotted us. Whatever it was, they had stopped doing it and were now staring as if they couldn't believe their eyes. Sam kept on walking and I kept trying to keep up with him.

One boy broke the silence. "Looka what's coming our way, guys. A gimp and a scarecrow."

Another corrected him, "A Jew gimp and a Jew scarecrow."

That got laughs.

The comedian called out, "Are you guys lost or just stupid? What're you doin' on our street?"

Sam kept getting closer and closer to the group. I was a step behind him, thinking that we should say nothing, keep our heads down, and speed past them.

Sam called out, "You don't own the street! It belongs to the City. Anyone can walk here. You have no right to stop us!"

What the hell is he thinking? I thought in a panic. Did he really want to get into a fight, the two of us facing the four of them?

Sam's words stunned the kids. Their mouths hung open as he came up to them and limped past.

He's going to get away with it, I thought, surprised.

I had just passed the group, still one step behind Sam, when I felt a hard thump on my back. Then more. A lot more. The boys had picked up rocks and were throwing them at us as hard and as fast as they could.

I hissed under my voice, "Run for it, Sam" but I knew as I said it that it wouldn't work. As much as Sam limped when he walked, his running was even more lopsided. The boys would become a wild pack, jeering and pelting us with rocks that would hurt more as they gained on us.

Sam knew it, too. He stopped abruptly. "No," he said. "We won't run." He yelled back, "This is not your street. We have the right to be here. If you don't like it, go to hell, you goddamn Guineas." Sam's words hung in the sudden silence.

I picked up a rock that had bounced off my back. I was angry but not at the Italian kids. At Sam. Why was he egging them on? He would be useless in a rock fight, not nimble enough to pick up a rock then straighten up and throw it hard. I would have to defend both of us.

I saw the four boys raise their arms to throw more rocks at us. I raised mine to return fire, thinking that, even one against four, I might be accurate enough to do some damage. I was very good in Pinners. I aimed for their faces.

Suddenly, a woman yelled, "All of you, drop those rocks! Right this second or else!"

CHAPTER TWO

All six of us turned as one. Two of the kids ran off at the sight of the small woman at the top of the stoop, her hands on her hips, a flour-dusted apron around her ample shape.

"Drop those rocks! Jimmy, Joey, now!" Rocks crashed to the sidewalk. Her finger pointed at me. "You, too, son! Drop that rock." The rock slid out of my hand as if it was desperate to obey. "That's better. Now shake hands."

There was an awkward pause.

The woman added, "Once I see you're buddies, you can come in and have cookies fresh out of the oven. So, what are you gonna do?"

Another pause then we all moved cautiously closer and shook hands. We mumbled our names. The Italian boys were twin brothers, James and Joseph Giudice, so alike that for a long time I thought of them as JimmyJoe as if they were one person. That force of nature in an apron was their mother, Rose Giudice.

The diplomatic exchanges completed, we turned to Mrs. Giudice. She nodded, opening the door to the house. "Now, remember, you're all buddies now. Buddies don't fight. They stick up for each other. Come on in. The cookies are ready and I need boys to eat them." Her hand waved us up the stoop and into the cool hallway. "Into the kitchen!" She made a pushing motion.

She did not have to urge us. We followed the intoxicating scent of warm sugar and butter. I had never smelled anything so wonderful, not in our home where baking was way beyond my mother's distracted attention.

Mrs. Giudice pulled trays of cookies out of the oven. She explained that they were family recipes from her Polish and Norwegian parents and grandparents.

Polish? Norwegian? Italian? I didn't care where the recipes came from. I watched her lift golden-brown disks off the trays with a spatula, putting them neatly on a big dish. An older girl worked by her side. She was introduced as Connie, the twins' oldest teenage sister. Connie took a jug of milk from the Frigidaire. While the door was open, I had caught sight of stacks of Pyrex containers in bright colors, with nary an empty space on any shelf.

JimmyJoe's mom urged us to try each type of cookie. As we ate, Sam and I mumbled answers to her questions.

Who were our people?

Our people? I wasn't sure what she meant so I said I was Michael Friedman and Sam was my cousin, Samuel Golden.

She nodded, "Ah, Jewish kids from the blocks over behind the Church?" We nodded back.

How long had we lived in Columbus Park?

Sam and I looked at each other. *Forever?*

What grade were we in?

That one I knew. I was going into sixth grade. Sam mumbled he was going into eighth.

When Mrs. Giudice looked surprised, Sam explained that, due to his polio, he had lost a year at school. She shook her head and brushed a gentle hand along his shoulder. Then she ordered the twins to tell us about themselves.

Joey (or was it Jimmy? I was not yet sure who was who) told us that they had moved into the house right after the last school year had ended.

The house? I glanced around in wonder. They had a whole house? For one family?

Joey, the talkative one, grinned proudly, "Yep, we need a whole house. There are six kids in our family!"

He rattled off their names and ages. I couldn't keep track except, like me, the twins were eleven years old and the youngest in their family. Then he got serious. "What's the school like? Are the teachers tough? Are the kids okay?" All the cockiness of the kid armed with rocks had gone.

He and Jimmy hung on my words. I thought how hard it would be to start at a new school in the sixth grade.

I never had to start over at a new school even though we changed apartments often. Usually we were asked to leave because people complained about my parents' fights. Or my father fought with the super over something or a neighbor asked too many questions about "our situation." Karen and I suspected that the real reason was that the rent was going up or Dad knew we were going to be tossed out soon. Some days we came home from school and were ordered to pack up, which we did quickly because we didn't have much of anything.

Despite the moves, Dad made sure we stayed in the same school district. That made life a lot easier. I was not any teacher's favorite, unlike my sister, who read all the time and did all her homework, but I wasn't a troublemaker either. Each year I went back to familiar faces. I knew which kid was friendly and which one was tough. I could predict what might happen at school more than I could foresee what might happen at home.

I offered, "I can show you around, especially The Park. There is a great pool and the Emmett playground and a good ball park." The quiet twin Jimmy nodded.

"Cubs or Sox?" Joey suddenly blurted out.

That was an important test. Which baseball team you root for is a big deal in Chicago where families split over loyalties. I racked my brain. *Had they mentioned where they had lived before?*

I took a stab. I knew that Taylor Street was where lots of Italians lived. Most likely White Sox territory so I said, "Cubs? No way!"

Sam's mouth hung open. He knew I was a steadfast Cubs fan, like my Dad. We put up with a lot of crap because of it. You had to suffer a lot as a Chicago Cubs fan back then because of how badly they played. I figured the truth could be revealed later when we knew these kids better. Sam closed his mouth and did not spill my secret.

Joey high-fived me across the table, almost knocking over his milk. I glanced at Mrs. Giudice. Would he get a smack for his almost-accident?

She was smiling, her hands clasped across her chest. "Boys," she asked, "would you like to stay for supper?"

Sam said, 'No, thanks.' He was expected home. His whole family sat down together for a dinner, just like the families on TV.

I had no such expectations, so I said, "I can stay! Thanks!"

"Do you need to call home?" Mrs. Giudice asked.

I hesitated. "There...there isn't anyone home. My dad works late and my mother is busy with stuff she does out of the house." I grabbed another cookie to avoid looking at Sam. Or Mrs. Giudice. I was sure she would know I was lying.

It was true that my father was at work. If I knew for certain that he was already home, I would have called, but, at that hour, my mother was usually the only one home. I knew the phone would likely just ring and ring.

If Mom did pick up, she often did not get who was talking or what they said. She wrote messages as poems, changing the names or facts to make them rhyme. She paid no attention to time, so she wouldn't worry if I was not home for dinner. Usually she didn't make any dinner so I wouldn't miss much anyway.

Mrs. Giudice's blue eyes studied me but she just said, "Boys, play outside 'til dinner is ready."

Sam left and headed back up the street. He walked with confidence. The street kids saw he had come out of the Giudice house so they knew he was part of the neighborhood now.

The twins and I went to the front stoop where we began Pinners. In those years I thought every boy in the US played Pinners. Later I found out it was only a Chicago game. Balls were pitched against the edge of a step. The scoring was like baseball. Depending on how the ball was caught or missed, and where it bounced, it could be a run, a single, an out, and so on.

As in all sports in Chicago, players argued over the scoring. I conceded to the twins because it was their home and their stoop. It was still fun.

When the front door opened, Connie yelled, "Dinner!"

The three of us raced to the bathroom to wash up, jostling for room at the sink. We squirted each other by squeezing our fists hard so that the soap shot up. We flicked water from our hands at each other's face. We laughed and nobody yelled at us to be quiet.

The table in the dining room was huge. There were three other Giudice kids already around it before the twins and I sat down. Mrs. G and Connie kept moving between the dining room and the kitchen so that the door between the two rooms didn't stop swinging. They brought in long loaves of bread, warm from the oven, and big bowls of spaghetti in a tomato "gravy." The food was passed up and down the table and the kids loaded up their plates, taking as much as they wanted. It was never like that in my house where food was measured out on each plate by Dad so there would be leftovers.

Mrs. G checked our plates when she sat down. "Michael, do you have enough? Connie, give him another slice of bread to sop up the gravy. Mangia, mangia, kids."

I copied the way the twins used soup spoons to hold the pasta as they twirled the long strings on their forks. We laughed when the last slurp of spaghetti whipped red sauce onto our faces. I tried to keep up with the twins but I was not used to so much food.

Then Mrs. Giudice served the main course!

There was a bowl of string beans seasoned with garlic and a platter of thin slices of beef "braciola" rolled around bread crumbs and other stuff and cooked in sauce.

I had never tasted anything like it before. My dad, who cooked most nights, fried or broiled chicken, fish and meat which were served with frozen fried potatoes and vegetables out of cans. Or he made scrambled eggs or grilled cheese sandwiches. Period.

This was heaven! The hot, spicy and juicy flavors exploded in my mouth.

Mrs. G smiled as she watched me while she smoked a cigarette and sipped a glass of beer. I smiled back because I wanted her to see how happy I was.

She gave orders. "I need someone to finish up the braciola. I do not want to be left with two slices on the plate. Joey, put one on Michael's plate."

She pointed to the oldest boy at the table, a silent giant, "Junior, take the last slice. Jimmy, you like string beans. Finish them up. Good, good." She put the cigarette between her lips, grabbed the empty plates and disappeared through the swinging doors.

I whispered to Joey, "Don't you have to save some food for your dad?"

Silence descended as all the kids looked at me. Joey shook his head, "Nah, Pop eats out most nights cuz of work. Besides, when he is home, he expects fresh. He never eats leftovers."

The door from the kitchen swung open again. Mrs. Giudice appeared with a platter of grapes and slices of watermelon. I thought I could not swallow even one grape, but the cool watermelon felt just right sliding down my throat.

I watched the twins spitting seeds at each other whenever their mother turned her back. I laughed for no reason except that I felt happy.

Then the doorbell rang.

CHAPTER THREE

When Mrs. Giudice opened the door, my father was there, dressed in his workpants and shirt with the label over the left breast pocket that said "Veriflex." He looked hot and angry.

He struggled to speak politely. "Hello, I am David Friedman. Is my son Michael here?"

Mrs. Giudice smiled up at my tall father, ignoring his scowl. "Mr. Friedman, I am very glad to meet you. I am Rose Giudice. We are new to the neighborhood. Michael is such a nice boy and the same age as my twins. They will be in school together so Michael can show them around. Won't you come in and have dessert? Or perhaps a cold drink, some red wine with fruit?"

Dad shook his head. "No, thanks. Michael stayed here without permission. I'd no idea where he was. I had to call Sam, my nephew, and ask where he last saw Michael.

"We have been over the rules, time and time again. Michael must ask if he wants to be out at dinner time or later. He cannot impose himself on others. He cannot roam the streets willy-nilly."

"Impose himself? He did no such thing." She put her hands on her hips and said firmly, "That boy is no imposition. In fact, it would be a favor to me if you permitted him to be here often. I can see already that he will be a good friend for the twins, a good steady friend, just the kind they need. They are too much together, just the two of them. That way, you wouldn't need to worry about him roaming willy-nilly, as you said."

My father looked over Mrs. Giudice's shoulder at me, sitting at the table between Joey and Jimmy. His Adam's apple bobbed up and down. He looked down at Mrs. Giudice. "If he agrees to call home to let us know where he is, he can be here at your invitation. But, Mrs. Giudice, if it gets to be too much for you, send him home. I do not want him to be an imposition."

She started to say something but instead she glanced at me and smiled. She looked at my dad. "I agree. He will call home so you know where he is. Definitely, he will phone home each time."

My father finally faced me. "Michael, say 'thank you' and come on home. It's late."

I said good-bye to the twins and waved at the others at the table. I stopped in front of Mrs. Giudice. "Thank you, Mrs. Giudice. It was great."

She kissed my head. "It was a pleasure having you here." Then she laughed. "Wait! I have some things for you to take home." She turned back to my father. "I made too much food. You must take some with you." She scurried away.

I stood uneasily by Dad's side, wondering what awaited me when we were finally alone. He did not speak. Instead he gazed around. The kids at the table stared back at us.

Mrs. Giudice reappeared with a basket of packages. "Some leftovers," she announced. "Some braciola and a few cookies and a bunch of grapes. Enjoy! I hope to meet your wife soon."

Dad's jaw tightened as he stared at the basket. I thought that he might refuse it, insulting Mrs. Giudice. Perhaps, she wouldn't let me come back.

He took it. "Thank you, Mrs. Giudice. Michael will bring the basket back when he is next here. But I'll be uncomfortable if every time he was here, you sent him home with food." She nodded that she understood. He added, "Perhaps you will meet my wife someday."

I knew that was unlikely to ever happen.

My father didn't say anything as we began to walk, so I tried to fill the silence. I left out the rock fight but I told him about the games of Pinners and I counted off the names of the kids in the family. I did not tell him about the fresh-baked cookies and the delicious food at dinner and how I could eat as much as I wanted. Talking about that would make him angry because it was so different at our home.

That thought led me to confess, "Dad, I knew I should have called but Mom gets so confused. You know how she is...." I let that hang in the air. He knew how she was. We walked on in silence.

Dad finally said, "Michael, it is okay with me if you go over to play with the Giudice boys and have supper when Mrs. Giudice invites you. But you must promise me one thing." He looked down at me, his brown eyes serious and his lips tight. "You don't stay if Mr. Giudice is home. If he comes in while you are there, politely say you must go home. Do you promise?"

"But I don't understand."

"You do not have to understand. You just have to do it. If Mr. Giudice is home, don't stay. Do you promise?"

I knew Dad. He wouldn't give me any reasons. I had to follow his rules or risk his belt so, of course, I said "yes."

CHAPTER FOUR

When we got to our building, I looked up as I always did, hoping it would be a good night. But there was no light shining through the second-story window.

The evenings when I saw a light or heard the radio were good ones. It meant my mother was feeling better, was out of the bedroom and was perhaps trying to cook or clean. Maybe she would sit down to supper with us and be interested in what was going on in our lives.

The darkness upstairs told me "Not tonight."

As we climbed the stairs, we passed Mr. Connelly's door. Usually the radio or TV was blaring a ballgame and we would hear Connelly curse or throw something. Other times, he would lie in wait for us then fling the door open and complain. Like he did that night.

"Friedman," he yelled. Mr. Connelly yelled all the time. "Friedman, tell your kids to stop stomping around like a herd of elephants."

"Connelly," my father said. "The elephants are in your head. They'll be gone when you stop drinking."

"Dirty Jew!" Connelly bellowed.

"Irish drunk!" my father shouted as he pushed me up the stairs, stomping his feet all the way, just to annoy Connelly.

When we went inside our apartment, my father sighed. The only light in the big room that was both living room and kitchen was from the setting sun. If Mom was home, she was in bed. If Karen was home, she was on her bed, reading. Karen was always reading.

"Evie," he called out. "I found Michael. He's safe." He added under his breath, "If you care."

The bedroom door opened a crack. My mother peeked out, her eyes red from crying. "Michael?"

"Yes, Mom?"

"Dad said you were missing. Were you?"

"Nah, Mom. I had dinner with friends."

"That's nice." She shut the door gently.

Dad sighed and emptied the basket Mrs. Giudice had given him. He looked at the braciola, not sure about it, then put it in the Fridge. He started making eggs for dinner. The way he slapped the pan onto the stove and slammed the cabinet doors shut, I could tell he was angry. I wasn't sure if it was at me or at Mom.

When he sat down at the table, Karen crept out of her room to eat with him. I sat down too.

Dad looked at me. "You can't still be hungry, Michael. Not after eating all that food at Mrs. Giudice's. She's Italian."

I wasn't sure about the connection between "all that food" and Italian. Dad must have seen my confusion, so he added, "Italian women feed their families well. Taking care of their family is important to them."

The unspoken words hung in the air over the table. *Your mom is not like that.*

I felt bad for Mom, so I added, "She's not Italian." Dad's eyebrows went up. I added, "Mrs. Giudice, I mean. She's Norwegian and Polish."

"Really? I didn't know that the Italians mixed with others." Dad turned back to his dinner.

"Dad?"

"Ah huh?" he asked as he folded the paper to the sports page.

"Why can't I be there if Mr. Giudice is home?"

Karen sighed her know-it-all older sister sigh.

"Michael," Dad said, with his "no more questions" sternness. "That's my rule. I expect you to listen." He must have felt bad that his words sounded harsh so he added, "How 'bout you get some of those cookies Mrs. Giudice baked?" He turned back to the sports pages and groaned, "Goddamn Cubs. They break your heart every season."

He got up and washed his plate and put it in the drain. Then he went into the bedroom to change into his other work clothes. I heard mumbled voices, my father saying something to my mother and my mother barely saying anything at all.

When my father came out, he closed the door hard behind him. He was dressed for his second job "to make ends meet." He said, "Michael, Karen wants to go to the library so you must stay in tonight. Your mother is not well. Understand?"

I nodded as he left. Karen drifted back to "her" room which was half of the room we shared with a partition between our spaces. She collected her library books and headed out.

I sat by the front window as the room got darker, listening to the sounds of kids playing outside. I knew what would happen next, now that Dad had left.

The door to my parents' bedroom opened and a wedge of light shot out. "Michael?" my mother said softly. "Can you bring me a cup of tea?"

"Sure, Mom."

The door closed gently. She would never ask me when Dad was home. It would set him off.

When the tea was ready, I put one of Mrs. Giudice's cookies on the saucer. Carefully balancing the dishes in one hand, I opened the bedroom door.

My mother was sitting in bed, looking worn out. As usual, the bedcovers were tangled and covered with paper. Her poems. She always scribbled poems, often the same one over and over. There were dark shadows under her eyes and wisps of hair hung limply around her face.

She motioned me closer. I handed her the tea and pulled the bedroom chair nearer the bed.

She pointed at the cookie. " Did Dad bring this home?"

I wondered how much I should tell her. How much would be too much? Mom got confused easily but I was still excited about my new friends and the amazing dinner I had eaten at their home, so I tried. "Sam and I met some new kids, twins who live near The Church. JimmyJoe Giudice. I had dinner with them. There was so much food that Mrs. Giudice sent stuff home when Dad came to get me."

"That's nice," she said in the flat way she spoke when she was very tired. I couldn't tell if she understood what I had said but I knew from her voice that she would be back in the hospital soon.

I don't remember if, when I was eleven, I knew what my mother's illness was. I know now that it was Gaucher's disease. It is already lurking in my DNA to be passed onto my children.

There are several types of Gaucher's but the most common type, Type 1, is found most often in Ashkenazi Jews, whose ancestors came from Germany and Eastern Europe like ours. Living in small villages, where everyone was somehow related, a genetic mutation, like the one that causes Gaucher's, spread widely.

Now, one in sixteen Ashkenazi Jews is a carrier. Carriers do not have the disease. It is a recessive trait so children of two carriers have a 1 in 4 chance to get it. All the children of someone with the disease will be carriers, as Karen and I are.

Patients with Type 1 Gaucher show symptoms early in life. Their bodies fail to produce an enzyme needed to break down a substance called glucocerebroside, so it builds up in their body. That causes bone pain and bone loss, reduced red blood cell counts and an enlarged liver and spleen. All this leads to bruising and fractures and extreme fatigue and jaundice. The only treatment back then was to transfuse the blood to reduce the anemia and to use analgesics like aspirin to treat the pain.

The emotional toll of the disease can often be worse than the physical. That is how Gaucher's affected our family. My mother's family kept it a secret from my father and my father never forgave them for it.

My parents met in Chicago during WWII. Dad was a GI, a tall handsome Jewish farm boy from Indiana, on leave in the big city. My mother was a beautiful young USO volunteer. They had a whirlwind romance, fueled by the looming separations and dangers of wartime.

Even though they married quickly, there must have been time for the truth to be told, if Mom's family hadn't worked so hard to hide it. It might have been shame or it might have been hope that kept them from telling my father. When Dad found out, the secret, as much as the disease, damaged their relationship.

How did he learn the truth? I'm not sure. Was he suspicious at my mother's reluctance to go to the doctor to find out why she was always tired? Was it the several years of marriage with no pregnancy?

They saw specialists who said that, if she conceived, it would be a "miracle," given her condition, her Gaucher's. Karen was obviously the first miracle and I was the second.

Once the truth was revealed, however it happened, their marriage was scarred. Dad knew that Mom's family had hidden from him the fact that she had a disorder that would make her weak all her life. And beyond that was the deep sadness that had plagued her starting in her teenage years.

In his anger and his hurt over the secrets, Dad refused to speak to Mom's family. He would drop Mom, Karen and me off for visits with them and pick us up hours later in front of their house.

Gaucher's left Mom weak which led to falls giving her bruises and fractures. Her fatigue left the house a mess with no food on the shelves, in the Fridge or on the stove.

That led to screaming tirades from Dad who arrived between his two jobs to find breakfast dishes still on the table and no dinner ready. Their arguments and Mom's bruises made neighbors report Dad to the landlords or the cops. Landlords asked us to move on, which we did, hopeful that, in another place. the stares would be less harsh or judgmental.

Karen and I tried to help. Many days, we washed the dishes, made our own lunches and tried to start dinner, just so there would be less tension when Dad got home.

When we could arrange it, we were not home when Dad first arrived. Those first minutes at home were the worst. It was as if Dad hoped each day that a miracle had occurred, that the rooms would sparkle and shine and smell of food cooking. That Mom would greet him, dressed like a TV mother, in a pretty dress and a crisp, clean apron with a big bow in the back. Dad's disappointment made him quick to get angry at everything.

Sometimes though, especially after a hospital treatment, Mom would be up and dressed when

Dad came home. She would say cheerfully, "Dave, how was your day?" And sometimes, there was food simmering in pots and laundry neatly folded. On those days, Dad's eyes lit up.

"Evie, today was great!" he would announce.

As we ate dinner together, Karen and I would look back and forth between our parents, just listening as they talked. We could see what had connected them long ago at the USO.

But, most often, if Mom was out of the bedroom, she would be at the table with her poems scattered around, focused on writing another one, her head bent close to the pad. No food was cooked, no laundry folded. The disappointment drew dark lines around my father's eyes and across his forehead. His jaws clenched over the rush of angry words.

I always hoped that my mother would not say anything. I prayed that she was aware enough to not goad Dad into yelling. But she never learned.

That was the other part of our "situation." Mom did not live in our world. She lived in her head, where words swirled and danced. She did not recall how the real world worked. Even on her better days, it was if she was a first-time visitor who did not understand the customs of the natives. She would suggest impossible things like she would say brightly, "Dave, let's have dinner out and a movie! Wouldn't that would be nice?"

"Evie, we can't. I have just two hours before I need to get to my second job."

"Oh, Dave, why do you always have to work? Play hooky today. Let's have some fun."

Karen and I would make our ways as quietly as possible to our room. Dad had built a partition with a door to make two tiny rooms out of one, my room leading to Karen's. Karen quickly got lost in a book. I put my pillow over my head and hummed, trying to drown out the angry sounds, but it never really worked.

My father would say in a tight voice, which meant he was wrestling to keep his anger under control, "Why do I always work? Why? Because we have bills, Evie, bills for your treatments. Last month, you were in the hospital for three days to get transfusions to build up your cell count. Then there are the visits to the rheumatologist for the joint pain and the orthopedist for the fracture in your arm. That's why I work all the time. Don't you remember?"

"But, Dave, it is not my fault."

That would do it! Dad's voice got loud and I heard him pacing. "No, it is not your fault and it is not my fault and it is not Karen's or Michael's fault. But who will take care of the mess we are in?

"You? You're their mother, but can you even keep track of when the kids are home and when they aren't? Do you make sure they have clean clothes and food to eat? No, not even that.

"So, who is left, Evie? Who is left in this goddamned family to take care of everything? Me! Just ME! And you don't even remember why I work all the time. Give me a break, Evie. Come down to earth and live here with us for a while."

Then Mom would run off to her room, crying, "I just thought we could have fun as a family." The door of the room would slam behind her.

There would be a pause before Dad started banging something like his fist against the Frigidaire or a skillet against the stove top. He needed to bang until his anger was gone. When he finally stopped, I would leave my room and sit with him while he ate and read the newspaper before leaving for his second job.

CHAPTER FIVE

A few days after the rock fight, Sam and I met JimmyJoe in the lot between the synagogue and The Church. Dad had okayed a trip to The Park if "you boys stick together and stay on the main paths."

Of course, I promised.

It was another blistering day. We planned to stay cool by swimming in the pool. I always swam in shorts. Dad said, swim trunks were a waste of money. How often do you need them and how different were they from shorts anyway?

We went into the locker room. The other guys changed into their trunks. I was there because Sam had to take off the brace hidden under his pants. He put it in a locker then leaned on me until he got into the pool. There the water helped him stay upright and appear normal.

The pool was crowded with kids from school. I introduced the twins all around. My pals were surprised that I had Italian friends from over on Gladys but soon nobody thought much about it.

We splashed each other for a while then Jimmy asked me to race him. I tilted my head towards Sam, clinging to the edge of the pool. Jimmy nodded and raced Joey instead.

The truth was that I was the one who couldn't swim. I always stayed in the shallow sections near the edges. Sam could do a good crawl with his strong arms, but he stayed near me so I didn't look like such a loser. Sam was good that way, letting guys think it was his polio that kept us both pinned to the wall.

When we were all waterlogged, we spread towels on the pavement around the pool to dry off and warm up. We stayed away from Karen and her giggly girlfriends. She was just as happy to be as far away from me as possible.

Eddie Cohen joined us with a bag of new comic books. My father called Eddie "the poor little rich kid," like Richie Rich in the comics, because he had lots of spending money but was always alone with "the help" in a big house right across from The Park. His father was a doctor and his mother was busy with "good causes." Dad thought Eddie had a bad life but I thought it was neat that Eddie could buy all the new comics when Finkelman's first got them and that his parents didn't always yell or hit him with a belt.

I introduced him to the twins and we sat reading and passing the comics around. Before Eddie left, he handed me comics to "borrow" for a few days. He didn't care if I gave them back all wrinkled from reading them over and over or even if I returned them at all. He always was buying new ones anyway.

Joey asked suddenly, "Did you guys go out for Little League?"

Sam and I looked at each other. Back then, Little League was competitive. There was none of the "everyone gets a chance to play" attitude. You tried out and you were picked by one of the coaches or you didn't get to play.

I answered, "Not yet."

Sam said nothing. We both thought, *what coach would want a kid with a leg brace?*

Joey had an idea. "We were in Little League last year and we want to get into the Junior Pony League next year. 'course if we had stayed in the old neighborhood, we'd have gotten onto a team easy but Ma said it was too far for her to drive us to practice and games and all. We'll need to try out again. We plan to practice a lot so we'll get picked. How 'bout we practice together?"

Jimmy nodded in agreement, but he always agreed with Joey. I thought, *how neat to have someone always backing you up.*

Joey added, "Tomorrow, bring your mitt over and we'll practice. Then, come spring, we can all try out for the Juniors."

Mitt? I had no mitt. I already knew what Dad would say, "Mitt? Another thing you don't need. You'll get tired of this like you have with everything else. You probably won't make a team.

You can't just waltz onto a Pony team, never having played baseball at all."

Jimmy said quietly, "It'd be great if we were on the same team."

I felt good about that at least. Jimmy hoped I would be with them as much as I wanted to be, although I couldn't see it how it would happen.

The twins began rolling up their towels, getting ready to leave. I felt awkward. Mrs. G had told me to come over whenever I wanted. I wanted to go now but could I just trail after them as if I was just another kid in their family?

Jimmy solved that with the kindness I had begun to expect from him. "Hey, guys, Ma said that you were to come for dinner, if you were available." He looked as if he really hoped that we were available.

Sam said "no" again. But I was available! I would always be available for lots of food and lots of laughter.

When we got to their house, we went into the kitchen to see what was cooking. Mrs. G was stirring a pot of "gravy." She picked up a cigarette from a big red ashtray and said, "You boys look like something the cat dragged in," but her smile said it was fine. "You must've had a good time."

We nodded, looking eagerly at the big cookie jar shaped like a white-haired grandmother. "You have to shower before you can have a snack. Joey, Jimmy, loan Michael some clothes. I'll hang all your wet things on the line. Get going, JimmyJoe Michael!" She ran all our names together, like the three of us were all connected.

We ran upstairs. The twins got into the shower together. It was so natural. They were brothers. Even more, they were twins.

Jimmy motioned me to join them. "The faster we shower, the sooner we can have snacks and I'm starving!" he declared.

It suddenly felt natural for me to get in there too. I was almost the exact same age, only eight days older. I felt like a brother. Mrs. G had called us, JimmyJoeMichael, the three of us, almost triplets. And I was interested in getting showered fast to get to the cookies.

When we were dressed in dry clothes, Joey showed me how to ride the bannister downstairs. We each did it, jumping off at the end.

Jimmy whispered, "Remember, we do that only when Pop isn't home. We'd catch it bad if he saw us."

We...us.... Like I was family! I filed this new family rule in my memory.

As soon as I got into the kitchen, Mrs. G reminded me that there were rules in my real family. She pushed me towards the phone.

"Hello, Mom. It's me. Michael. Nothing is wrong. I am having dinner at the Giudices'. My friends. The twins. I told you. Yes, I did."

The twins were listening. So was Mrs. G, although she kept stirring the gravy and checking stuff in the oven.

"Mom," I said, getting annoyed. "Dad said it was okay to eat here as long as I called. Will you tell him that I called? Can you write it down? Mom, please remember that I called."

After hanging up, I waited to let my cheeks cool before I turned around. When I did, Mrs. Giudice just said, "We are having fish tonight, Michael. We have fish on Fridays. Will you eat it? I know some kids who don't like fish."

Joey made a gagging sound. Jimmy laughed.

She continued with a smile, "I got one of those fish-hating kids right here. I made lasagna, too, so fish haters can have that instead."

I didn't love fish but I thought that Mrs. G would make it better than Dad. Boy, was I right! Mrs. G's fish had a topping of breadcrumbs mixed with cheese and green herbs. It smelled great when she brought the dish to the table.

But first there was a big bowl of salad and some warmed bread with butter and garlic. As we passed those around, a car door slammed.

Everyone became still. The oldest brother, Junior, was holding the salad bowl, about to take a portion. Instead, he put it on the table and placed the serving fork and spoon back in it.

I looked at Jimmy, wondering what was going on. He mouthed, "Pop's home."

Mrs. G took off her apron, crushed out her cigarette and patted her hair. She stood at the door as it opened and Mr. Giudice stomped in.

The old expression "built like a fire plug" fit Mr. Giudice to a T. He was short with no neck, but had broad shoulders, huge hands, and a waist as wide as his chest. His face was round with froggy dark-brown eyes. He seemed hard—hard to know, hard to like and hard to please. Despite the July heat, the room had gotten very cool.

Mrs. G said, "Evening, Lou. Good day?"

Mr. G grunted and went into the kitchen, Mrs. G following right behind. We heard the tap run and murmurs of voices. Nobody in the dining room said anything or took a breath.

The dining room door swung open as Mr. G tossed the towel on the counter in the kitchen and entered. Mrs. G padded after him, her slippers making a soft slapping sound.

He looked around, as if taking attendance. His eyes landed on me. As he sat down, he asked, "Who's the skinny kid?"

Mrs. G said hurriedly as she put a place setting in front of him. "That's Michael Friedman. He showed the twins the pool in Columbus Park today so I invited him to dinner."

Mr. G nodded. "Friedman? Jewish? That's good. Listen, kids. Jews are smart. The best accountants and doctors and lawyers are Jews. You can learn a lot from Jews." He looked at Junior and tapped the table with his forefinger. The silverware chimed with each jab. "Jews work with their brains, not their backs or their fists, cuz they're smart. A Jew won't flunk out of school, spending his life loading trucks. Nah, they'll be in the office, figuring out how to make a business look like it's losing money. They're smart. You can learn a lot from them."

He stopped to give everyone time for his words of wisdom to sink in. He sighed like he had no hope that they would. He ordered, "Food!"

The food traveled up the table, passing kids along the way but no one took anything. When the bowls and platters reached him, Mr. Giudice helped himself, then nodded. The kid next to him took the platter, spooned out a portion then passed it on. No one said anything or looked up as they ate.

Mrs. G didn't sit. She and Connie went back and forth, bringing in the food then the wine that

Mr. G called Dago Red. He poured himself a large glass, took several swallows then slammed the table with his fist. Everyone stopped eating.

He growled, "Giuseppe! Why is there no fish on your plate?"

I knew that Joey was Giuseppe because his face had gone white. "Pop, I don't like fish. Ma said I could have lasagna instead."

"Well, I say that everyone eats what was bought with my hard-earned cash and that your mother spent hours making. Giacomo, pass the fish back to your brother."

Jimmy silently passed the platter to Joey who put some fish on his plate. His father stared at him until he put a piece in his mouth and swallowed it with a big gulp of water.

Just then the phone rang. I had a flash of hope: Dad was calling to order me home. Home seemed a lot better right then. Dad had told me to leave if Mr. Giudice was there but I didn't know how to do it without it being rude.

Mrs. G answered the phone. She pushed the kitchen door open and said, "Lou, for you."

When Mr. G went into the kitchen, Mrs. G waved her hands to encourage us to eat. She patted Joey on his head and put a gentle hand on my shoulder.

Mr. Giudice came back a few minutes later but he didn't sit. Instead he drank down his glass of wine, then said, "Business. I have to go. How much do you need, Rose?"

He dug into his pocket and took out a thick roll of bills. He peeled off one after another until Mrs. G nodded then he left, letting the front door slam behind him. We heard the car engine start followed by the crunch of tires down the alley. The engine's roar grew softer as the car went further down the street.

It was then that everyone let out the breath they had been holding and started to eat again. But all the laughter had disappeared.

After dessert, I said to the twins, "I have to go home now."

I went into the kitchen where Mrs. G was leaning against the countertop smoking a cigarette and sipping beer. She looked tired but she smiled at me. "How are you, Michael, dear?"

"I'm fine, Mrs. Giudice," I said, matching her smile. "But I have to go home now." I paused feeling that I had to explain more. How to explain the situation at home? "My mom doesn't always remember things so I don't want her to worry that I got lost somewhere."

Mrs. G smiled gently then straightened up. "I almost forgot. Wait here a moment."

I heard her slippers slapping softly up the stairs. There were sounds of things opening and closing before the steps came down again. Mrs. G appeared, carrying a big laundry bag.

"With so many kids, I need more space in closets and drawers and that. You are thinner than Jimmy and Joey so you might fit into these. There are some of Connie's things for your sister. Hardly worn at all. You would really help me out if you took them. Both of you can keep what you like. Give away the extras to people who need them." She handed me the heavy bag.

I was worried that it would seem like charity to Dad and he would get angry. My worries must have been written on my face because Mrs. G. reached over and put her hand under my chin to make sure I was looking up at her. "Michael, you will help me a lot by putting these clothes to good use. I hate to waste anything—food or clothes or time. Make sure your dad knows that I *begged* you to take this bag to help *me* out."

She kissed me on the head and gently pushed me to the door.

CHAPTER SIX

Dad was home when I let myself in with my key. He was at the table, reading the newspaper, dressed in regular clothes. Karen was there with a book but she wasn't reading, just staring at it.

Then I remembered. It was Friday night. Dad's second job was in Mr. Greenbaum's factory. "A religious Jew," Dad called him with respect. The company was closed on Friday nights and Saturdays, the Jewish Sabbath so Dad was off those days. He was off many Sundays as well unless Greenbaum needed him to fix machines so that orders for steel file cabinets did not back up.

Dad had shadows under his eyes. "Michael, sit down." He pushed my chair out with his foot. "I have to tell you kids something."

As I sat, I muttered, "I called, Dad. I phoned home that I was eating at the Giudices'. I wasn't sure that Mom understood what I was saying."

Dad nodded. "I know. I saw a message by the phone that said, 'He called.' But Mom's not here now. That's what I must discuss. Michael, Karen, your mother has not been feeling well for a while. When I got home, I found her on the floor, crying in pain. She didn't know why. She couldn't explain anything to me."

He looked down at his hands resting on the paper. "You know what happens when she falls.

She gets bruised and sometimes she breaks a bone." He sighed. "I took her to the hospital. She will stay there for a few days. People will be coming to the house to talk to you. They think…."

I knew what they thought. This had happened before. People always suspected that my mother's injuries were the result of Dad's rages. Gaucher's was not well-known outside of a few specialists who worked with Jewish patients. I just hoped no one who was "concerned about" my mother's injuries spoke to Mr. Connolly. He would say bad things about Dad. Other neighbors had in the past. That's why we had to move.

"What is that?" Dad had spotted the laundry bag near the front door.

I explained how Mrs. G needed more room in her house. Karen looked up when I mentioned clothes from Connie.

Dad shook his head. "She needs our help? Well, right now with all the medical bills…." He heaved a big sigh. "I'll have to figure out how to pay her back. Let me know if there are any repairs she needs done."

Karen piped up. "Can I look in the bag?"

Dad nodded so she dragged it into her half of our room. I heard her pulling things out, uttering "oohs" and "aahs" at what she found, while throwing the boys' stuff onto my side.

Dad seemed softer at that moment. I didn't want to miss the chance so I said quickly, "Mr. Giudice came in while we were about to eat. I couldn't leave, Dad, without insulting him."

He nodded so I went on. "It was strange. While he was there, no one talked, no one moved."

"I understand that it would have been hard to leave without it getting a lot of attention, without it being insulting. Just remember what I said. If you find out that Mr. Giudice is at home or if you see a big black car outside, don't go in. Say your mother needs you. Okay?"

It was a nice conversation, so I dared more, "The twins are going out for the Junior Pony League in the spring. I want to as well. Can you get me a mitt and practice with me so I can make a team? Just throw the ball around with me for a few minutes each day."

Years washed away from Dad's face. "Did I ever tell you how much ball I played in Indiana? God, I loved the game. I was pretty damned good. Yep, I was a damn good catcher until I broke the fingers in my left hand. I loved it."

He looked at me as if he was seeing himself in me. He added softly. "Let's see about getting you a mitt so we can practice. Let's see about getting you ready for a team come spring."

I wished he could run out that night or the next day to find a mitt but things did not happen like that in our family. Anything that cost money came slowly.

My father talked to my mother a lot about money. Mostly he yelled at her a lot about money. As I already said, she would go out for one thing and come home with a thing that no one really needed. Or she would come home with a new dress or hat or a pair of shoes.

She always showed them to Dad as if she was proud. She never remembered how angry he got, how he asked her sarcastically where she got the money to buy it. She always said innocently, "Dave, I didn't need money. I got it on credit."

Dad would yell again about "credit." "Dammit, Evie. That does not mean it's free. They expect the money back in payments. They charge interest so we wind up paying more than the thing is worth. Take these things back now, while the tags are still on, before you wear them."

Mom would cry and wring her hands. "I'm sorry, Dave. I wanted to look nice for you." She would say that over and over.

Sometimes she remembered to take the things back but, if she didn't do it right away, she would cut the tags off. Then the dress or hat could not go back. That seemed the only part of Dad's lecture

51

she remembered: if the tags were off, you can't return the clothes.

The rest of us knew we had to save up for most things. It was good that Dad was clever with his hands so he could buy things cheap then fix them up. He found a second-hand car and made it run like new. He fixed radios and toasters and even a TV so we had those too.

But there was nothing to fix on a baseball mitt. I worried about how long it would take Dad to get me one, about how long we needed to save up for it, about not having time to practice to be good enough to get on a Junior Pony team. That was going to be hard anyway since I hadn't played Little League.

But it turned out not to take long at all. That was how much Dad loved baseball. And perhaps me too.

CHAPTER SEVEN

The next day, as Dad had predicted, a lady and a man came to speak with Karen and me about "our home life." I hated the way they spoke softly to make us trust them. Dad had to sit in the bedroom so we "could speak honestly about what bothered us." I wish I could tell them that what bothered me was that my mother did not live on the same planet as we did.

We answered all their questions. Just like we had answered questions for the others who visited after my mother went into the hospital or to a doctor's office with bruises and fractures and was not sure why she was there or how she got injured.

Each time people came to the house, my father would ask if they had checked her records. He would show them letters from doctors and articles on Gaucher's that explained how easily patients got bruises and fractures.

They would respond, "Mrs. Friedman cannot tell us how she got her injuries."

Dad would sigh. "Of course, she can't. She gets confused or she forgets things when she's tired from the Gaucher's. After she gets a transfusion, she has good days again."

The investigators finally shut their pads, clicked their pens closed, snapped the locks on their briefcases and left. Dad told us to stick around. He wanted to go to the hospital to check on Mom. Afterwards, he said, we could do something fun. That's why I stayed put and didn't sneak out to hang out with friends.

Karen and I hoped that the something fun would be a movie. We never went into the Loop to the big movie houses to see the new films. Those were expensive theatres that people got dressed up to go to.

Instead, we went to the theatre on Madison, just four blocks away so we didn't even have to pay bus fare. The movies weren't the latest so tickets cost less. Since we didn't go to the movies often, we usually hadn't seen the film.

Karen looked up the movie listings. They were playing *The Ten Commandments.* We both wanted to see it.

We often snuck in snacks to the theatre because Dad said the stuff there cost too much. We usually stopped at Finkelman's where we picked out boxes of candy then hid them in our pockets. My favorite was Atomic Fireballs which almost burned my mouth each time. Karen liked M&Ms which she sometimes shared even though she never wanted one of my Fireballs in return.

I had a great idea. Dad could take the twins with us to pay Mrs. G back for being so nice. That way he didn't have to feel bad when Mrs. G had me over for dinner or sent me home with stuff. Karen pouted at that but perked up when I said that perhaps Connie could come too. That way, she could thank her for the "new" clothes.

The day turned out better than I had hoped. When Dad came home, he had a mitt.

"We were in luck," he said. "Reiner's had one in the window. I went in and bargained for it."

Reiner's was the secondhand store around the corner. Most of what we needed came from there.

The glove was a four-fingered model, no longer popular with players. But that didn't matter to me...yet. What mattered was that Dad was excited he had found a mitt for me fast and at a good price.

It fit perfectly and the leather was soft. Dad said that way you really felt the ball.

He rummaged in the closet and came up with his old mitt and a scuffed-up ball. I didn't know he had those hidden away. I didn't know he had played the baseball in Indiana and been real good at it.

We went out to play catch at the edge of The Park where there was an open field. I wasn't good at first but Dad was patient...for a while.

I got better as I got the feel of the glove. Dad gave me pointers on how to improve my throw and a few times, my throw hit his glove with a real "thwack." He took his glove off and shook his fingers, blowing on them like they really hurt, then he laughed. Those were great sounds—the thwack of the ball into his glove and his laugh.

On the way back, we walked down the twins' street. There was no black car in the alley. Dad motioned me to follow him as he climbed the stoop and rang the bell. When Connie answered, my dad asked if Mrs. Giudice was at home.

I heard the soft flip-flop of her slippers as she approached. "Come in, Mr. Friedman," she said, holding the door open.

Dad said "No, thank you." He just wanted to ask permission to take Connie and the twins to the movies that night. "My treat, Mrs. Giudice," he said. "You have been very kind to my kids. I want a chance to be kind in return. Fair's fair, after all. If you won't accept a favor from me, then we can't accept favors from you. Capisce?" He winked and she laughed.

That night, at *The Ten Commandments*, I sat between Joey and Jimmy in the row right in front of Dad. He wanted to keep an eye on us, the three boys, JimmyJoe Michael. We each felt the jab of his finger when we spoke or laughed too loudly. Karen and Connie, the goody-two-shoes, had chosen seats at the other end of the row to be far away from their brothers and their "cooties." We were just as glad being away from their giggles and sighs over the "dreamboats" in the film.

As we said back then, it was a gas. The theatre was cool and, as I shared my favorite candy with the twins, I had only one more wish. I wished Mom was there too.

CHAPTER EIGHT

During early autumn, Dad and I played catch after dinner before he had to leave for his second job. He even gave up reading the sports pages while he ate so he could finish faster and start practice while we had enough light.

Some nights, the twins came by and we all practiced together. Dad would bat a few balls at us so we could get fielding practice and he would let us take turns batting as he pitched to us.

He gave us pointers to improve our skills. I was proud that the twins saw how swell a player he was. He told us how he was the catcher for his high school varsity team in Indiana. Only I knew he had been the only Jew and caught hell because of it.

I wanted to play the same position. I had an ace up trying out for a team because Dad could teach me all he knew. How he would be proud of me if I followed in his footsteps.

JimmyJoe, however, were better at everything we did during practice. That made sense since they had played Little League before, but I still felt lousy when Dad said, "Watch how Joey grabs the ball from his mitt. Fast. Every second counts in a game" or "Good hit, Jimmy. That would be a double at least." I didn't want Dad to think I was a loser at the game he loved. If I didn't make a team, these times with him would be over.

We often walked back to our house together, Dad, the twins and me. I was uneasy because our apartment was small and bare compared to the whole house the twins' family had.

Worse, if my mother was home, she came out of the bedroom and greeted us. She poured us glasses of Kool Aid or just plain water, if she hadn't bought anything else. She opened a bag of store cookies, if we had them. If not, she took out bread and smear jelly on it, if we had any bread or jelly. She cut the crusts off and made the bread into fancy triangles, but it was still not fresh-baked cookies and cakes.

After their first visit, when I walked the twins to the front door, Joey asked, "Why is your mom that color?"

I tried not to sigh out loud. Mom was always yellow but, when the poisons backed up in her blood, the yellow got very dark.

I said, "That's just how she is," and shrugged.

Mrs. G taught me a better answer.

It happened one afternoon when I went to the Giudices' house to call for the twins. Mrs. G. answered the door, dressed not in a house dress and slippers but in a nice dress, with her purse over her arm.

"Hello, Michael," she said, surprised. "Didn't the twins tell you that they had Catechism today? No? They must have forgotten."

My disappointment showed because Mrs. G added, "I have an idea. Would you help me do my shopping? I am hosting a christening party for my new niece. I need a strong boy to help with the packages. If you aren't busy, that is."

That was a kind way to ask. I said I would be glad to help her. Mrs. G led me around the house to the garage where she kept an old red and white station wagon. She slowly got into the driver's seat while I hopped onto the passenger seat. She moved the seat forward as far as it went and wiggled a pillow behind her back so she could reach the pedals.

Finally, we set off...slowly. Mrs. G drove with the window down so that her cigarette smoke blew out of the car.

We wound up on Cermak Road in Berwyn. I got out of the car to signal her as she parked ...slowly. Then we walked slowly up the road, Mrs. G. dragging one shopping cart on wheels while I pulled another.

All the stores had Italian names. Mrs. G. stopped at many to buy their specialties. We went to the cheese store for mozzarella and what she called "gravy cheese." We stopped at the pork store for sausage and other meats. The butcher cut the chops and roasts just the way she wanted, weighing each piece and wrapping it in paper, marking the package with a thick stubby pencil.

Next, we went to the fruit and vegetable store. Mrs. G. pointed to each tomato, zucchini and eggplant she wanted, one by one, as the "fruit man" chatted with her in Italian like an old friend.

From there we went to the bakery where she bought breads and fancy cookies. The cookies were packed carefully in a white box formed by the shop girl from a flat piece of cardboard. She pulled a red and white string from a spindle dangling from the ceiling, wrapping the string quickly around the box, crisscrossing it along its width and length and tearing it off with a metal hook on her finger to tie a bow knot. Just as we were about to leave, Mrs. G asked for "a sample" for her nephew to taste.

It took me a second to realize that I was the "nephew." I took the cookie that was offered by the shop girl on a piece of waxy tissue paper. It was a crunchy tube of fried dough dusted with sugar and filled with a sweet creamy cheese. One of the best things I had ever eaten!

I whispered my thanks to Mrs. G as I licked the sugar from my fingers. She turned to the shop girl. "Clearly, they are delicious. Look at Michael's smile. Please deliver six dozen assorted Saturday morning."

Mrs. G really needed my help. At each stop, bags or boxes or parcels wrapped in paper went into our carts. Mrs. G opened her purse and pulled out a roll of bills to pay. Soon, our two carts were filled and heavy to pull.

As we made our way back to her car, she made one last stop. At an ice cream shop! She asked me to pick out whatever I wanted.

As I dug into a black and white sundae with fudge sauce and wet walnuts, she asked, "Michael, how's your mother? The boys said she's been ill."

I nodded, eating a big spoonful of ice cream, so I had an excuse for not talking.

Mrs. G was not to be put off. "I guess that she has jaundice. That must be why her skin is yellowy. Poor thing."

I nodded again, looking down at my sundae.

Mrs. G said softly, "Illness strikes every family, Michael. It is nothing to be ashamed of. My sister suffers from liver disease and, when she has a spell, she turns yellow and must have transfusions. Is it like that for your mother?"

I nodded and because there was no more ice cream in my dish and because Mrs. G was so easy to talk to, I told her what I knew about my Mom's disease and how she had to go to the hospital often. In an explosion of words, I said how my Mom got so confused at times that my Dad would get angry about her being in her own world and about all our money problems and how she made our home so confusing that I didn't know what each day would bring.

Mrs. G. touched my hand. "Of course, Michael, it is hard for you and your sister and your Dad. Try to remember that none of this is her doing. She must feel bad that she can't be better. It is difficult to want the best for your children but to not be able to make it so for them."

I gulped back my tears. There had been no one to talk to for so long. I whispered, "My dad would hate that I told you about our family's problems, especially the bills and all."

She rubbed my hand. "I am good at keeping secrets, Michael. Each family has secrets." A sad look washed over her face. "I know how good it feels to be able to talk about what bothers you.

"You can talk with me anytime you want. I will not tell anyone what you say. Not even the twins."

Then she added, "But it is up to you to tell the boys about your mother's illness. You can just say, 'My mother has an illness that makes her skin yellow. Often she goes to the hospital for treatment.' If you say it like that, the boys will just shrug it off. They know their Aunt Angie gets transfusions too so it is not strange at all to them."

I thought that over as we walked back to the car with the heavy shopping carts creaking behind us. I was a big help that day, loading groceries into the trunk and folding the carts so they fit in too. I helped by carrying the groceries up the stoop and placing them on the kitchen counters. Mrs. G looked up at the clock shaped like a big cat whose tail moved to the seconds. "My, my. I need to get dinner started. Would you like to stay to eat?"

I wanted to get home to keep Dad company. I didn't want him eating alone. I wanted to throw the ball around with him.

Mrs. G watched as these thoughts marched through my head. She handed me five dollars. "For all your help today, Michael. Spend it on something you really want." She kissed my head. "Remember. I am a good listener and an excellent keeper of secrets and I am always here." She laughed. "Always in the kitchen, cooking!"

On my way home, I stopped at Finkelman's and bought Mom a hand lotion that the bottle claimed smelled like roses. I bought Dad a Sports Illustrated magazine. I found a 'Teen magazine that Karen would love. And I bought the latest Superman comic just because it was what I really wanted.

CHAPTER NINE

Shopping with Mrs. G became my weekly job. Each Wednesday, after school, when the twins were at Catechism, I rode with her to the markets, then dragged a cart behind me as we went in and out of the shops along Cermak. Sometimes I had the only cart if there was no special occasion that weekend or if Mrs. G had done shopping already that week. But she always paid me five dollars.

If there wasn't much shopping to do or she didn't need to go to the market at all, I helped her in the kitchen. She taught me how to cook Italian. I chopped onions and garlic then cooked them slowly in olive oil so they got soft but not burnt. I opened large cans of Italian tomatoes in juice and dumped the contents into the pot. Then we added the herbs and red wine vinegar and a pinch of sugar. The "gravy" sauce would simmer slowly to be used later in lasagna or eggplant parmesan or just tossed with pasta for a first course.

As we shopped or cooked together, we talked about school and families, mine and hers. I knew that I could tell her everything…almost… and the twins would never discover my secrets.

I told her how I wanted to get on the same team as JimmyJoe but I was afraid that I wasn't good enough. She patted me on the shoulder and told me to keep practicing with my dad.

I confessed that I was jealous when Dad spent time practicing with the twins. He could see how much better they were than me because they had played before and practiced a lot more than I did.

She shook her head. "The twins only practice with your dad, Michael."

I was surprised. "Doesn't Mr. G throw the ball around with them? Doesn't Junior?"

She shook her head again and lit another cigarette. She folded her arms across her chest and looked out the window to the backyard. "Lou doesn't have time for the twins. He has less time for the family these days. Junior too. He now works with his dad. So I am glad that your father gives the boys time. It's important for them to have a man around." She took a drag and sighed. "There is so much here that a man should do...."

I felt her sadness. "What do you need done, Mrs. G? I could help you."

She smiled at me. "I think fixing the dryer is a bit too much for you."

"My dad can fix anything," I said and, because it sounded like bragging, I added, "It's true! He buys secondhand stuff and gets it to work like new. Even our car! He bought a 'lemon' then, as he says, he made it into 'lemonade' by fixing it. He can fix your dryer...."

"I don't want to impose on him. He has little free time and with your mom not feeling well...."

But I remembered. "You said to my Dad I was not 'an imposition' when I stayed over for dinner. You said it was a 'favor' when I did that. Dad will say the same thing. It is not an imposition to help you. It is a favor to do something for you since you do so much for me."

She laughed and ruffled my hair. "Very clever! Okay, ask your Dad but I won't be angry if he doesn't have time to do it. Mr. G gives me plenty of money. I can call a repairman."

Dad grinned when I told him about that conversation. He had been angry about Mrs. G giving me five dollars each week because he couldn't afford an allowance like that. Now he could repay Mrs. G for all her favors.

On Saturday, when he told Karen that we were going to the twins' house, she said that she had been invited to come over, too.

My mouth dropped open. "Invited by whom to do what?" I demanded.

She tossed her head and said that I should close my mouth because I looked like a dead fish then explained. Connie had invited her when they were sitting together in the movies. Connie was studying in beauty school and she wanted to practice on Karen's hair.

All of us walked over together. Karen disappeared with Connie. I joined Jimmy and Joey for Pinners outside while Mrs. G. showed Dad the way to the cellar where the dryer was.

Other kids from the block joined in the game and so did Sam. There were plenty of arguments about the score. Time passed quickly so we were all surprised when mothers on the block started calling their boys home for lunch.

Mrs. G came to the door and said, just as if we were all one family, "JimmyJoey Michael! Wash up then go out back for lunch." She waved her hand at Sam. "Sam, you too! Get washed."

On the patio table, under something she called a pergola, Mrs. G had spread a checked cloth and put out a pile of sandwiches and a bowl of potato chips. There was a big pitcher of lemonade and one of iced tea. My dad was there already, wiping his hands on a towel.

"Mangia! Mangia!" Mrs. G ordered so we all sat down and grabbed a sandwich. She lit a cigarette and poured drinks, then sat next to the twins. Dad was across the table next to Sam and me. Karen and Connie took their food and sat on lawn chairs by themselves. Too cool to eat with us, I guess. I never told Karen but her pony tail with a big curl in it looked neat.

We guys kept talking about sports as Mrs. G kept checking that we were eating enough. When she brought out fresh-baked chocolate chip cookies, she no longer needed to watch that we were eating enough.

She asked, "Dave, how much do I owe you for the dryer parts?"

Dave?

Dad waved his hand. "Now," he said in a tone that was firm, not angry, "we discussed this. I needed to pay *you* back, Rose."

Rose?

"Lou doesn't like people doing favors for him if he hasn't done anything for them first."

"Rose, I'm not doing a favor for *him*. I'm doing one for you. You have done lots of good things for Michael and for Karen."

That was the end of the discussion then but it resumed later when our doorbell rang at night.

Late night visitors were never a good thing for our family. Dad and I looked at each other. Karen lifted her head from her book. Mom emerged from the bedroom, looking worried.

I could tell from Dad's look at Mom that he was worried that she had put too much on credit and not told him...again. It had been a long time since a bill collector had shown up at our door but, if Mom's memory was turning bad, who knew what the bills could be?

And Mr. Connelly was still crabbing about the noise he claimed we made. Had he complained to the landlord? Was it the landlord at the door ready to evict us? I didn't want to move to another apartment on another block now that I had made friends with the twins. And Mrs. G.

Dad went down to the door while I stood at the head of the stairs, watching. Mr. Connelly was at the door of his apartment, holding a beer bottle. His TV boomed behind him. He groused, "Friedman, now you're having visitors in the dead of night. Ain't you got respect for others' peace and quiet?"

"If you want peace and quiet, Connelly, turn down your damn TV," Dad said automatically, his focus on the door. The bell had rung again and now there were loud knocks, once, twice, three times.

When Dad opened the door, Mr. Giudice was there, dressed in a shiny black jacket that bulged over his belly. He demanded, "You Friedman?"

Dad nodded.

Mr. G put his hand out. " Lou Giudice! You fixed my dryer?"

Before Dad answered, Mr. Connelly muttered, "First the Hebbes, now the Wops."

Mr. G spun towards Connelly. "Whaddya say?" he growled. "Say it again, louder, so I can hear you good."

Connelly stepped quickly back into his apartment and closed the door.

"Too bad you have such crap neighbors," Mr. G shouted at Connelly's door. "Some folks need to keep their mouths shut if they ain't got nothing good to say." There was no sound from behind Connelly's door except the blaring TV. "And some folks need to turn down their goddamn TV if they know what's good for them." The TV went silent.

"Better," Mr. G. muttered and turned back to Dad. "So, Friedman, you been repairing stuff?"

"I repaired the dryer for Mrs. G, I mean, Mrs. Giudice," Dad said. "She's been good to my kids so I was glad to do her a favor. I don't like to always be on the receiving end of favors."

Mr. G nodded while he took out a wad of bills. "I won't argue about paying you for your time, seeing you wanted to do Rose a favor but I'll pay back the money you laid out for parts. Just so's you know, I can get those parts for cheap in my line of work."

"Your line of work?" Dad asked, then looked as if he wanted to swallow his words.

Mr. G. studied him for a moment, then he said, "I'm AAA Sewer Repairs. I dig them, clean them, repair them for contractors, for the City, for the County or for a lucky Joe Shmo. And anything related to them such as septic tanks, pumps, pipes, and that. Anything backs up into your house, I'm the man to call. Water in the basement? Call me. Anytime you need pipes or hoses or pumps or parts, I'm the man. If you help Rose again, just yell for the parts you need. I can get them real cheap. For Rose or for yourself. Understand?"

When Dad nodded, Mr. G added, "And if you need extra work for extra cash, no questions asked, let me know. I have jobs where I can use an extra pair of hands and a good head. Your people are smart. Your people and my people, we got a lot in common. New to this country. Love our families. Work hard to get ahead here." He raised his voice. "And we have to deal with assholes like your neighbor who don't know enough to keep their mouths shut." He peeled a ten off his roll of money and tried to hand it to Dad, who shook his head "no."

Mr. G looked at me, wadded the bill up and tossed it towards me. It fell just a few steps up. He said good-night then turned and left.

Dad stared at the closed door. I said hesitantly, "Mr. G seemed nice, didn't he, Dad?"

Dad said to the door. "Michael, if you see a black car in the alley or in front of the twins' house, you don't go in. If you see a truck marked 'AAA Sewers,' you don't go in. Understand?!"

I did understand now. Something had twisted in my gut when Connelly turned off his TV at one comment from Mr. G. I stepped down the stairs to pick up the ten-spot.

CHAPTER TEN

All winter, I practiced throwing and catching, hitting and fielding with Dad. along with the twins. Even if it was icy or snowy or football or basketball season. I had one goal: April tryouts. I just had to be good enough to be on the twins' team. Or any team, for that matter.

Suddenly it was April. The tryouts for our district were held on a Saturday morning on a ball field in The Park. All the coaches of the local teams were there as well as lots of parents. Dad was there but not Mr. G so Dad rooted for all three of us. JimmyJoe Michael.

We lined up, counted off and were sent into the field or into a batting line-up. The boys on the teams last year were guaranteed spots this year, so they threw to us new guys to field and to hit.

I fluffed a few balls I should have caught. I got desperate to show what I could do. I scrambled and dove for balls, slid into bases, and swung as hard as I could to get a hit, any hit. I wanted the coaches to see that I would work hard, even if I was not good enough right then and there.

As the twins and I walked off the field, Dad shook the twins' hands and rubbed my hair. He said, "You all tried hard, JimmyJoe Michael. Michael, you showed the coaches how much you want to play. Whatever happens, you tried."

That sounded as if he thought I wouldn't get picked. At least, he wanted me to feel good about trying out.

We waited to hear from the coaches. They met right away to discuss all the boys they had seen. Players might be wanted by several coaches so sometimes they divvied up the talent pool. Really good players might hear from two coaches so they could choose their team. Coaches then filled in with second choices later in the week.

Starting Saturday afternoon, phones rang all over Columbus Park. If a kid got a call early enough, he could pick up his team cap that day.

By Monday, several boys were sporting new caps. On Tuesday, Jimmy and Joe appeared at the corner on the way to school, proudly wearing the red caps of the Columbus Chiefs. I told them they looked "swell" as I swallowed my jealousy.

By Wednesday, more and more caps in different colors appeared at school. I began planning to be absent the rest of the week and dreaming of ways to avoid the whole baseball season after that.

I went over to the twins' house Wednesday after school as usual, glad the twins were at Catechism. It was hard seeing them at school with their caps. It was hard on them, too, trying to make it seem like no big deal that I hadn't gotten a call.

Joey said, "It's just kids' baseball. Lots of kids don't get on a team."

That didn't make me feel any better. Lots of kids didn't go out for a team but I had tried hard. I cared and Dad cared about it too. He had even checked the phone to see if it was working.

It was.

Mrs. G knew something was bothering me as we drove to Cermak Road. How could she not? I didn't anything during the whole trip and just shrugged when the lady in the bakery offered me a choice of cookies. Mrs. G didn't comment until we were unpacking the bags in her kitchen.

"Michael, dear, what's the matter?"

"Nothing, Mrs. G. I just don't feel like talking."

"I think it's the baseball teams. Am I right?"

I knew she would not stop until she found out so I spilled it all. "I tried so hard, Mrs. G. I practiced with Dad every day. I wanted to be on the twins' team so bad. Now, I might not be on any team at all." I blubbered a little bit.

She hugged me. I smelled her perfume and the smoky tang of her cigarettes. She said firmly, "It will work out, Michael. I promise it will."

I shook my head. Women don't get it. Things don't work out in sports just because you want them to. You get on a team because a coach spots your talent and he needs it to round out the roster.

If you are a pretty good catcher, but some other kid is a great catcher, he gets the call and you don't! That's just the way it is.

Mrs. G handed me a Kleenex just as I heard a van roar into the alley. I stiffened. The back door to the kitchen flew open and Mr. G appeared.

He was covered in muck that stunk so badly, my eyes watered. He didn't say a word, just disappeared into the basement. The twins had told me that there was a shower room there so that Mr. G could wash off without bringing the smells of sewers into the rest of the house. Since the laundry was down there too, he could throw his dirty clothes into the washer along with the wet towels. Mrs. G always left a change of clothes in the basement for him.

Mrs. G said, "Michael, I'll be right back."

She disappeared down the basement stairs. The rushing water from the shower made the pipes under the kitchen sink bang. Over the sound I could hear loud voices but Mr. G and Mrs. G might have just been shouting over the noise of the water hammering through the pipes.

Mrs. G returned, her face glistening with moisture. She patted a stray curl back into place. "Michael, I have extra eggplant parmesan here, left over from last night. I must make room in the Fridge. Do me a favor and take it home with you."

Every Wednesday, she needed to make room in the Fridge and I had to help her by taking food home. Now she added, "Try not to worry about the baseball team. It will work out."

Thursday came and went and there was still no phone call. My father ate the eggplant in the dark kitchen, not even bothering to turn the light on to read the sports pages.

I sat across from him, pushing food in circles on my plate. There was no point going outside to throw the ball around. My season was over.

I vowed not to play ball ever again and not to call on the twins either. They were excited about the season. I would spoil it for them by being gloomy and jealous.

When the phone rang before dinner on Friday, Dad let it go. Probably just bill collectors or the landlord with Connolly's complaints.

This time, however, Mom was making fish for dinner. She had opened a package of frozen breaded fish to bake with frozen French fries.

She stared at the ringing phone then, when Dad didn't make a move, she lifted the receiver. "Hello? Who? I don't know anyone with that name. What is this in reference to?"

My father rose with a groan and took the phone from her. "This is David Friedman. Who is this?"

His voice lifted, "Coach Fiorello? Yes, of course. It's for you, Michael. Coach Fiorello wants to talk to you."

Coach Fiorello? From the Columbus Chiefs? I grabbed the phone. I asked him to repeat what he said so I could be sure. "I made the team? Yes, yes. Of course, yes!"

I was a Chief! On the same team as the twins! The coach would have a cap for me at the first practice the next day.

Dad was grinning as I hung up the phone. We high-fived. My mother smiled. "Good news?" she asked.

"The best!" Dad said. "Michael made the team he wanted. He gets his cap tomorrow."

A thought flashed through my mind. All week, guys had paraded around the school wearing their teams' caps. I had missed my chance to show off. I was probably a second choice, picked after some better player had decided which team he wanted.

I shook off that moment of doubt. I had made the team! That was the important thing. I would have a whole season to show the coaches what I could do.

I thought of how Mrs. G knew it would work out. She had faith in me, even when Dad had doubts. Even when I had doubts. I wanted to run over to the twins' house to tell them and Mrs. G the news.

I couldn't. Mom was trying to cook so I had to stick around to eat dinner. Then Dad said, "Let's go out for ice cream after dinner to celebrate. Let's make it a family night out."

The next day, I raced down to the field. Coach Fiorello shook my hand and welcomed me to the team. The twins were there, beaming at me, as I put on my team cap. The Coach told us that we could pick up our uniforms at Govas Brothers Sporting Goods on Cicero Avenue next week. We didn't have to pay anything. Our team sponsor had covered all the costs.

The twins and I went down to the store together. They seemed as surprised as me when we got our shirts. On each one in letters filled with fancy curlicues was:

AAA Sewer Repairs

CHAPTER ELEVEN

Coach Fiorello turned out to be strict but fair. He laid down his rules during our first practice. Be on time. Bring your gloves. Be ready to play. Be respectful to the coaches and to your fellow players. We are a team, a band of brothers. We'll try to win, but, no matter what, we'll always stand up for each other.

That lesson came home right away. I had brought my glove, the four-fingered one that Dad gotten secondhand. Ronnie, a big kid with a big mouth, made a big deal about it. "Look at Friedman's lame glove. Where the hell did you get that? From a cripple with only four fingers?"

He kept it up whenever I missed a catch. His loud nasty comments would come fast after each fumble. Finally deflated with shame, I tossed the glove down and marched off the field. No way was I going to let the guys see me cry but I was close to it.

Dad was in the stands with Sam. Sam had tried out too but had not made a team, but, with his typical good nature, Sam was planning to help the coaches by keeping notes on the opposing teams and taking care of equipment and stuff.

Dad had brought a sandwich to eat so he could watch the practice then go off to his second job. When he saw me throw down the glove, he ran to me and hissed, "Get your ass back on the field, Michael. Don't you dare quit because someone hurt your feelings! If I could put up with being called a dirty Jew when I played, you can put up with crap about your glove!"

"No! I won't go back. You bought me a crap glove because you're cheap. You just couldn't pass up a deal. I won't play with a crap glove."

My father lifted his hand towards me. At least, he hadn't taken his belt off. He wouldn't dare whip me with the belt where others could see but I had felt its sting many times in our apartment.

Just then, Coach reached us, carrying my glove. "Mr. Friedman, let me talk to the boy."

Coach turned me to face him. "Michael, the glove doesn't matter. It is the hand in the glove that makes all the difference. Your glove was well-cared for. See how soft the leather is and how tight the seams. Whoever owned this glove before had respect for it. A player who showed that much respect and care for his mitt played the game the right way. There are probably great baseball games in its past. All that history is yours now if you respect this glove.

"Now get back on the field! Let's see what your hand in that glove can do!" As we walked back, Coach glared over his shoulder at Dad.

Dad watched silently during the rest of practice. When we walked home, all of us were very quiet, the twins, Dad and me. We waited as JimmyJoe walked to the door. Mrs. G opened it and invited us in for a cold drink.

Dad said, "No, thank you, Rose. Dinner is waiting for us at home."

That was not really true. We never knew if dinner was waiting, but the black car had been in the alley so Dad had no interest in a visit to the Giudices'.

As we walked across the Church's parking lot to our block, Dad finally said something to me. "Coach was right. Some people hunt for a weak spot to make a man seem small so they feel big. When I played ball, I had to learn to ignore the name-calling because I was the only Jew on the varsity team, beating the pants off the goyim.

"Just like Hammering Hank Greenberg. He showed the world what a great baseball player a Jew could be, but he had to hear some really bad things from the stands. And Sandy Koufax, another Jew, probably the best pitcher ever.

"So, as Coach says, it is not the glove on the hand that matters. It is the man who wears the glove that makes all the difference."

He reached towards me suddenly. I flinched. He paused, then more slowly, put his hand on my head. "When you get bigger, Michael, you can use my glove. I played great games with it. I would be really proud if you added more great games to its history."

When we got home, the apartment was dark. "Evie, you here?" Dad called out.

"Yes" came softly from the bedroom. But, for once, Dad did not follow that with angry words about not having any dinner waiting. Instead, he scrambled eggs and toasted bread for Mom, Karen and me, before leaving for Greenbaum's.

That night, I rubbed oil into my glove to keep it supple and wondered about the games its other owners had played. Perhaps it wasn't such a bad thing that it was secondhand. It had history.

April sped by with practice three times a week. No practice on Wednesdays, because most of the boys had to go to Catechism classes at Christ the King.

Sam came with me to each practice and spent time on the bench taking notes for the coaches. He would set up the equipment and give us cups of cold water from the big cooler Coach brought to each practice. It was clear that Coach Fiorello and the assistant coach liked having him around, so even Ronnie kept his mouth shut about Sam and his gimpy leg.

My mitt became so comfortable that I forgot I was wearing it. Coach said it meant that the glove had become one with me, different from being stiff and awkward like some new gloves could be.

When the season got underway, Dad told the Coach that he would drive kids to the away games. Some were in tough neighborhoods far away so rides with parents were important.

Dad's car was a green Chevy Belair he had rescued from the scrapyard and got humming like new. He loaded it up with kids and filled the trunk with our gloves and bats. When we arrived at the field, we scrambled out, like the funny cops stuffed into a tiny cop car in old movies.

Dad would sit in the stands for the whole game, eating a bag supper. Sometimes Mrs. G came with us. Dad insisted that she ride in our car especially if the field was in a "tough" area.

She argued, "I know 'tough.' My dad ran a bar and there were fights there every weekend."

Dad got that hard look in his eyes as he shook his head. That look meant, "Don't argue! Just do what I say because I will not change my mind." I guess Mrs. G got to know that look because she stopped arguing and just got in the car with us.

Mr. G never came. Neither did Mom.

I was kind of glad because Mom didn't get baseball. When we watched the Cubs on TV, she couldn't tell the teams apart even though one wore white home uniforms and the other team dark ones. She kept saying as a batter got a hit or a player tagged someone out, "That's good, right? That's good for our team?"

Dad would finally have enough. "Evie, stop it. You never get it. All you do is ruin the game for Michael and me. Find something else to do."

Her lips would quiver and she would clench her hands together. I changed my seat to be next to her and kept up a stream of whispers. "Our team is batting now. Gosh darn it, that looked like a ball but the ump called it a strike. That stinks. Now that one was a ball, way out of the strike zone, so far out the ump actually saw it. Great, a base hit. Run! Slide! Safe at first base!"

I high-fived with her. She laughed, perhaps still not understanding the game, but knowing I was on her side.

Mrs. G understood baseball. She couldn't avoid knowing the game because she had grown up above her Dad's bar where games were always on the radio and, later, on the TV. And she had four brothers who took bets on all the sports.

She would stand in the bleachers, not much taller standing up than the other fans sitting around her. She put her hands around her mouth like a megaphone and cheered. She would moan and groan and wave disgustedly at the umpires who, she insisted, were as blind as bats. When Dad stood next to her, he looked like a thin giant next to a short fairy godmother, but he never laughed at her because she really knew the game.

As we inched towards the playoffs, the twins' Uncle Jim, Mrs. G's oldest brother, began driving players to the away games in his big station wagon. The whole team fit into our two cars. Uncle Jim had a trumpet which he blew every time we scored or got the other team out. We had a whole cheering squad.

We made the first round of the city playoffs that season but lost to a team from Bronzeville. I was the last batter up but did nothing but fan air.

As we trudged off the field, cringing as the Bronzeville fans cheered their team, Coach stopped us. "Line up. Stand tall. Be good sports."

We lined up to congratulate the winning players. They said some nice things as they shook our hands, such as "Good game," "You almost had us in the fourth inning," "Hope to see you next season."

As we loaded our gear into Dad's car, Mrs. G poked her head into the window. "Let's go to Buffalo Ice Cream Parlor. My treat! And come to our house on Saturday for a barbecue. Bring your parents and brothers and sisters."

Dad opened his mouth to say something but we were cheering loudly, so he just closed it again without a word.

At the ice cream parlor, he argued with Mrs. G. over who would pay. She looked him straight in the eye, hands on her hips, her purse dangling from one arm. "You have driven boys to every away game, even as far as the north side. You stayed there for hours even when you had to eat dinner out of a bag. You work two jobs, Dave. You will not buy ice cream today. You have done enough. Now let me do my part."

Later, Dad admitted with a smile, "No way was I going to win that argument with her."

I didn't smile back. I was already worried about Mom going to the barbecue at Mrs. G's house.

CHAPTER TWELVE

I hoped that the barbecue was just only a momentary idea of Mrs. G but I should have known better. The phone rang a few days later when Dad was at his second job. I wasn't quick enough. Mom picked up the call.

"Yes, this is the Friedman's house. Who is this? Oh, the twins' mother? I know them. A barbecue? But why? Where? When? If Dave says it is okay."

When she hung up, I waited to see if she would tell me about the call. When she didn't, I asked, "Who was it, Mom?"

"The twins?" she said tentatively. "A barbecue? Saturday?"

The details were fading fast so I filled in the blanks. "Mrs. Giudice, the twins' mom, is having a cookout to celebrate our team's season. Saturday at their house. Did she give you the time?"

She shook her head. "Dave will know."

I hoped she wasn't going to go. I'd worry the whole time about her vagueness and her inability to hold a conversation. She was very yellow again. Perhaps she would be in the hospital? Then I felt terrible for thinking that.

When Dad came home, I told him about the call. He looked at my mother who was at the table, writing in her notebook. He didn't say anything but, after Mom went to bed, he called Mrs. G back.

"Rose, thank you for the invitation but Evie is not good in crowds, especially in an unfamiliar place with new people. But we will be uncomfortable, trying to keep an eye on her. Rose, can't you understand? Okay! What time? What can we bring? I insist. What is Evie's specialty? You still don't get it. A dessert? Fine."

He hung up with a frustrated bang. "I lost that argument too! She insists that your mother come. I agreed that we will bring a dessert."

The next day he told Mom, "Evie, we are going to the Giudices' home on Saturday."

My mother nodded without a word.

"Can you make a dessert? Something sweet?"

She tilted her head then said, "A Jell-O mold? I can make a Jell-O mold, can't I?"

Karen and I looked at each other. We knew we would probably have to make it for her. At least we wouldn't have to worry about it burning. Mom's baking attempts almost always ended in burnt cookies or rock-hard cakes because she forgot to set the timer or even remember that stuff was in the oven. Later, when we wondered about the strange taste or texture, we found a key ingredient, such as eggs or vanilla or even sugar, still on the counter.

Surprisingly, making the Jell-O dessert with Mom turned out to be fun. Even Dad pitched in.

At the local branch library, the librarian had found a cookbook from the Jell-O company for me. I stopped off at the market with my five dollars from Mrs. G to buy the stuff we needed.

The night before the barbecue, we made the "Italian Party" dessert with three layers of Jell-O: one green with canned pineapple, one yellow with tiny marshmallows and one red with maraschino cherries. Each color had to be mixed and added separately so the layers didn't bleed together. That was the hardest part, waiting for each layer to gel before the next step.

We sat around the table playing cards, waiting for the timer to ring. Dad had bought the timer to help Mom remember things in the oven but often she forgot to set it. We were there to remind her.

Mom was a fierce gin player. While she forgot many other things, she remembered all the cards that had been discarded and those that were collected by other players. She won many hands.

That night Dad lost often but he laughed when Mom teased him for throwing out cards she needed. He grinned when she reorganized her hand again and again, as if confused, then laid down "gin."

As they laughed and teased each other, I glimpsed the young couple who had married fast all those years ago, before Dad found out how Mom's family had hidden her problems from him. Before he knew that he would have only rare glimpses of that happy girl in all the years ahead.

Our Jell-O dessert looked real pretty. I held it carefully on a tray as we walked over to the Giudices' house.

Mom looked pretty, too, dressed in a summery dress in bright colors. Her hair was swept up on top of her head and she wore makeup and lipstick. Karen had helped her get ready with tricks Connie had taught her.

Dad held her by the arm as we went down the alley towards the sounds of people in the backyard. She hesitated near the gate. Dad gently pushed her into the crowd.

Mrs. G greeted us with a smile. She oohed and aahed over our Jell-O creation and put it on the dessert table near all the fancy cakes and cookies. Then she introduced Mom to the other mothers.

Dad watched her go off then let out his breath. I hadn't realized until that moment that I had been holding mine, too. Now I felt that things would be okay since Mrs. G had taken over.

The twins pulled me into a game of Pinners. Dad slid into a group of men moaning about the latest Chicago teams' disasters.

Mr. G's voice boomed over all the others as he clapped men on the back and kept ordering, "Eat, eat! Look at all this food Rose put out." And "Drink! Drink!" as he pointed to the kegs of beer and the pitchers of homemade wine. He manned the grill, flipping burgers, franks and sausages. "Eat! Mangia!" he ordered.

So everyone ate.

I had never seen so much food. All the stuff from the grill and bowls of coleslaw and potato and macaroni salads. Then, of course, all the desserts!

"Who made this?" Mr. G was pointing at our Jell-O creation.

Jimmy whispered, "Michael's mom."

Mr. G turned to Mom who was still seated where Mrs. G had planted her, with her uneaten food on a paper plate in her lap. She was stunned to be the center of attention.

He grinned. "You know, this has got to be my favorite dessert. The goddamn Italian flag in Jell-O!!" He clapped his hands, barking a loud laugh.

I let my breath escape. I hadn't noticed I had been holding it...again.

CHAPTER THIRTEEN

The early part of 1960 glows brightly when I look back on it now. All the good times stand out: shopping with Mrs. G, playing catch with Dad, making the team, almost getting into the playoffs.

For a few weeks in late September, while the professional teams were playing for the pennants, Dad and I still threw the ball around in the hours between his jobs. JimmyJoe would come to play catch too. Sometimes we would watch games on TV together, JimmyJoe Michael, the "triplets," all squashed together on the sofa, moaning as the Cubs' season ended early again.

Then suddenly the good times stopped.

Mom came down with what the doctor called "the flu." For days she stayed in bed, drinking fluids and taking aspirin. We made sure she did what the doctor ordered when one of us was home but she was on her own during the day.

One day, I arrived home first because Karen had detoured to the library to get new books. I heard crying from the bathroom. I found Mom lying on the floor in a pool of blood.

She couldn't tell me what was wrong. She kept moaning, her face a terrible shade of yellow, her lips bluish-white. Her eyes were closed but opened when I called her name. I filled the bathroom glass with water but she waved it away. Her eyes closed again.

I didn't know what else to do so I sat on the floor, hoping Dad got home soon. I worried, *what if the boss offered him overtime?* He never turned down overtime.

I went to the kitchen to phone the factory to ask Dad to come home right away. This wasn't the first time I had to make such a call so I knew Julie, the girl in the office, would be sure to get the message to Dad.

When he arrived, he looked at Mom still on the bathroom floor and ran to the bedroom. I heard him curse then rush to the phone. "Very bad, Doc. She's bleeding from down below. The aspirin bottle is empty. I don't know how many. She probably didn't remember so she took more whenever she saw the bottle." He sighed, "Can't we do something here at home? Okay, okay, call an ambulance." He hung the phone up with a loud crash and punched the wall.

Dad carried Mom to bed, after I laid towels over the sheets. He said, "The doctor thinks she is bleeding inside from too many aspirins. Her blood system was already weak and now with the flu and all the aspirins...." He scrubbed his face. "We were just getting back on our feet...."

Twenty minutes later, just as Karen got home, the ambulance arrived. Dad said, "Michael, Karen, go to Aunt Jennie's. I have to go to sign papers to get Mom into the hospital."

Karen nodded 'yes.' She and Sam's sister, Sherrie, were close.

I said, "Sam isn't home. He works at Finkelman's after school now. Can I go to the twins instead?"

"Okay, okay. But if the black car is there...." He didn't finish the sentence. Where would I go even if the black car was there?

It wasn't. The twins were playing out front but, after one look at me, they got their mom.

Mrs. G ushered me into the kitchen where pots simmered on the stove. "Michael, sit. What happened? Your mother?"

I started to cry. "There was so much blood."

The twins got very quiet. Mrs. G wrapped her arms around me and rocked me gently. She must have signaled for JimmyJoe to leave because I heard the kitchen door swing close.

"There now. Tell me everything," she soothed.

I cried as I told her how scared I was for my mother. And how scared I was of my father because I knew, when bills mounted up, Dad would feel that he was drowning again. He would

96

rage and curse Mom's parents for not telling him the truth, for hiding her illnesses. He would get angry about everything, pulling his belt off to whip me for any mistake. Because of the bills. And all the secrets in our family.

Mrs. G said only "There, there," until I stopped sobbing. She handed me a Kleenex to blow my nose and dry my eyes then she said, "Michael, I want to help. I will ask your Dad if you and Karen can stay with us for a few days while things settle down with your mother. You can sleep in the twins' room and Karen can share Connie's room. Would you like that?"

Would I? Of course, I would.

Mrs. G drove me back to our apartment. I was surprised because it was only a short walk across the parking lot between the Church and the synagogue, but she explained that her feet were so bad now that she drove everywhere. When she parked in front of our dingy building, I was too tired to care about how different it was from her neat, clean, bright house.

We climbed the stairs slowly because of her bad feet. Without a word, Mrs. G went to work. She cleaned the bathroom, stripped the bloody towels off the bed and bundled them into a pillowcase to take back to her house to launder. She opened the windows to let in fresh air.

She was washing the dishes piled in the sink, when Dad walked in. He got angry. "Rose, what the hell are you doing? I didn't ask for your help. Leave the dishes alone and go home."

Mrs. G folded the dishtowel very carefully and put it on the counter, then she put her hands on her hips and lifted her chin. "David Friedman, don't you dare speak to me like that! I am being a good friend. If you don't like to be helped, think of Michael. The poor boy is scared for his mother and scared of you because you take your anger out on him. That is not fair."

I gasped. Mrs. G had just told my secrets to Dad but he didn't care about that. He was too angry about everything else.

He yelled, "Fair? Life isn't fair and the sooner Michael learns that, the better. I thought life was fair once but I was a patsy, a fool, tricked into taking on someone else's problems. Now I am chained to working hard but getting nowhere."

Mrs. G. folded her arms over her chest. "Then take your anger out on those who caused the problem. Not on this boy. I am here because I want your permission to have Michael spend a few days at our home. And Karen too. That way, you can focus on what you need to do for your wife without worrying about your children."

Suddenly Dad stopped yelling. He stared at me huddled near Mrs. G. He took a deep breath. "Karen can stay with my sister and her family. Michael can stay with you until Friday. He spends Friday night with my folks.

"Michael, pack some clothes and your school stuff. Remember to be good. Help any way you can. I will come by each evening to let you know how your mother is doing."

I ran into my room to pack before Dad changed his mind. On my way out of the kitchen, I heard Mrs. G say, "Dave, isn't it time to ask her family for help? That is what family is for... to pitch in and help in tough times...."

I am ashamed to say that I often forgot why I was staying at the Giudices' because I had so much fun. JimmyJoe and I called ourselves "the triplets." I slept on a cot in their room in the space between their beds. We talked and laughed late into the night, unless Mr. G was home. If he was, he would bang on the door and yell, "Sleep! Or else!!!" We pulled the blankets over our heads and laughed, but never loud enough for him to hear.

The first day I walked to school with the twins, the ladies on the stoops asked, "Who's the new boy?"

One explained, "Oh, he's Rose's family."

They all nodded at that. I knew I was really accepted after I knocked over a trash can chasing a ball in another wild game of Pinners.

One of the ladies stuck her head out of her window and yelled in Italian, "Pick up all that trash or I will come down and knock sense into your wooden head."

At least, that is what JimmyJoe said it meant.

Dad stopped by each day on his way to his second job. He always told Mrs. G that he had just eaten when she asked if she could make him a plate. He said that Mom was very anemic from the Gaucher's and from losing all that blood so she had to get transfusions and stay at least until Saturday.

I knew from her past episodes that getting transfusions was like filling a car with gas. The more she needed, the more it cost. Each day she was in the hospital, the bills mounted up.

Dad never mentioned money worries to Mrs. G. Instead he thanked her for being good to me by bringing her a carton of her favorite cigarettes. That was a nice gift back in the day before the Surgeon General put warnings on each pack.

On Friday, he picked me up to go visit his parents, which I did every week. My bag was ready, full of clean and folded clothes. Mrs. G said she just threw my stuff in with the twins' to fill the machine when she was doing a wash so she didn't waste water or soap.

Dad didn't argue about the laundry. He had also stopped arguing about the food wrapped up in foil because she needed room in the Fridge. He had never won an argument with Mrs. G yet.

"Is Mrs. Friedman coming home soon?" Mrs. G asked.

Dad shrugged. "Perhaps tomorrow, the doctor said. They are checking her blood values today."

"Michael can stay next week. He is no problem at all. With all the kids, I don't even notice him."

"We'll see," Dad said. "Thanks again."

Mom did come home that Saturday. Dad helped her up the steps to our apartment and tucked her into bed. She looked less yellow but she was still weak.

When I went to her, she hugged me and said in a whispery voice, "I am glad to be home, Michael."

"I am glad you are home, too, Mom," I said back and kissed her on her cheek.

I *was* glad. But more than that, I was happy to see that Dad was glad she was home too.

He brought her a cup of tea and handed her her pills. "Now, Evie, swallow these. Then you should rest a bit before eating. Karen is reading in her room and Michael and I will be outside, playing catch, so the apartment will be quiet."

I was glad about that too. It had been a long while since we had had a catch.

"And," he added with a twinkle in his eyes, "the season is over for both Chicago teams, so Connolly won't be blasting his TV." He pulled the covers up to her chin then we left the room.

As we got into the rhythm of catch, Dad made comments before each thrown ball. "Michael, we all need to work together to care for your mom. We can't just leave pills with her. She forgets how many she takes so we must hand them to her at the right time. When I'm not home, you and Karen will need to do it." He launched a fast throw at me.

That meant I wouldn't be going to stay overnight at the twins'. I threw the ball …hard.

Dad stretched to reach it. "Michael, I am going to work Saturdays at Veriflex. We need money for all the bills."

I had to move fast to catch the ball that time.

"Zayde and Bubbe want to have you and Karen to stay over the whole weekend, not just Friday nights."

That wasn't bad news. I loved staying with Zayde and Bubbe, Dad's parents. Zayde let me stay up late to watch comedy shows and boxing matches. We sat side by side, crowded tightly into his big arm chair, sucking on his favorite candy, big sour balls.

Bubbe was always in the kitchen, just like Mrs. G, but Bubbe cooked potato latkes and kugel, chicken soup with matzah balls, gefilte fish, and baked goodies like Mandelbrot and babka. All the recipes she said were real Russian Jewish recipes made the old-fashioned way so they were *geschmacht*. By which she meant 'tasty' in Yiddish.

But spending time with Zayde and Bubbe and staying home in the afternoons meant being away from The Park and the twins. And Mrs. G.

So, I whined, "Dad, I like going over to the twins'. I like helping Mrs. G. on Wednesdays. Can't I still do that?"

Dad tossed the ball a few times into his glove as he thought. "Michael, you can go to the twins' house in the time between my jobs. But either you or Karen need to be home when I leave so that Mom is not alone. Since the Pony League season is over, you have to stay home if Karen has school activities." He added, "Invite the boys over to our place. You can watch TV or hang out in your room."

He heard my sigh. "I know it's hard, Michael, but family members have to help each other when they're needed. Mom needs us now."

I got angry at that. "What about Mom's family, Dad? Her parents? Her sister? Only your family helps out! It's us or Aunt Jennie and Uncle Bernie and Sam. And Zayde and Bubbe. It's not fair."

"No, it's not fair, Michael. That's life. Some people have it easy. They can turn away from the problems right in front of them and still sleep well at night. I can't do that. I bet you can't either."

"And Mrs. G can't too!"

"You're right. Mrs. G is one of the good guys who can't turn away. But she has her own family to worry about. Now watch it, Michael. This will be a fast ball."

I jumped up high to catch the throw but something went very wrong. I crumbled to the ground, screaming in pain.

Dad rushed over. "Don't get up. What is it? Your right foot? Let me see if anything is broken. Doesn't seem to be. Perhaps you twisted your ankle. Let's get home to ice it." He tried to make me feel better by saying, "You're just like the guys in the majors. Making a big deal when all they really need is to put ice on it."

I couldn't put any weight on the foot. Leaning on Dad, I hopped up the stairs. He filled an ice bag and held it on my ankle. He joked, "I should open a hospital. I have a patient in each room."

Karen came out of her room to see what was happening. She winced when she saw my face. Even sitting down, I was in pain.

Dad ordered me to take it easy. He let me use his TV chair and brought me grilled cheese sandwiches to eat from a folding tray. Karen huffed at first at this special treatment but then she saw I was in too much pain to enjoy it.

The next day, Dad massaged my foot. He said to "walk it out" but the pain was still too much.

He sighed. "Lie down on the couch. I'll get a heating pad. Sometimes heat works better."

By Monday, the pain had transformed into a dull throb that I could ignore at school. I even played Pinners with the twins on their stoop until the pain grew so bad, I started missing easy catches. I was glad I had to go home so Dad could leave for Greenbaum's.

When Dad left, Karen went off to a friend's to work on a project. I was stuck at home to make sure Mom took only the right pills. Good ol' Sam came over to keep me company.

As Sam slowly climbed the stairs, Mr. Connolly stuck his head out and muttered, "I thought so! It's the gimp."

I thought, *My pain is nothing to complain about.*

CHAPTER FOURTEEN

On Friday night, Dad took me over to the Montrose section of Chicago, where Bubbe and Zayde lived near a lakeshore beach. When we arrived, Zayde and Bubbe were arguing. Zayde was helping clean for Shabbos but, when he dusted what he called a "tchotchke" and put it back on the shelf, Bubbe would cluck at him, "Nein, nein. Not there. Here! What do you think?"

Zayde rolled his eyes. "There? Of course, there. So much better, right, Michael?"

They always argued about everything then threw up their hands and laughed. Like when they played cards, they would roll their eyes and say, "What you think? That I want that lousy card. What you don't know would fill an ocean." And one or the other of them would look at me and wink like we were conspirators. I loved sitting there, listening. "Kibitzing" they called it.

After Dad left, Zayde said we should walk the boardwalk before dinner. "For some fresh air," he said. "Good for the lungs and the digestion."

I tried to ignore the pain in my foot as we started off. The beach ran along the shore of Lake Michigan and people were out in the sunny fall weather, walking, running, biking. We sat for a while on a bench, watching the boats on the lake. If you turned sideways, you could see the tall buildings of "The Loop." There was no Sears Tower or Hancock building yet but the brand-new Prudential Building pierced the sky.

As we stood up to walk back, I gasped in pain.

Zayde grabbed me. "Tatele, the foot again?"

It wasn't. This was a new pain. In my back. I flexed and twisted. It subsided a bit.

We walked slowly back to the apartment, where Bubbe greeted us. "Nu, what took so long? You are suddenly not interested in eating? Abe, you didn't spoil Michael's appetite with the junk they sell on the boardwalk, did you?"

"Sure, I fed the boy all the crap I could find. What you think? I have no brains in the head."

They were off arguing again but grinning at the same time. All the while, Bubbe was putting out the challah warm from the oven and plates of roasted chicken with squares of steaming kugel smelling of onions.

My mouth watered. I leaned in for a forkful. Ping! Pain shot up my back. My eyes teared.

Bubbe patted my shoulder, "Slow, Michaeleh. Not so fast so you don't burn your mouth."

I didn't tell her what the real problem was, but I told Dad as soon as he picked me up late Sunday. By then, I was worn out with the throbbing pain in my foot and the stabbing pain in my back.

"Okay, okay," he muttered, more to himself than to me. "A few aspirin and some stretching and you will feel better."

On Monday morning, when I tried to get up, I had to sink back into bed. That's where Dad found me when he came to check on why I wasn't at the breakfast table, dressed for school.

"I can't, Dad. My back hurts too much."

He asked, just to be sure, "You don't have a test today? Is there a bully you want to avoid?"

I shook my head. He studied me for a moment then left my room. I heard him speaking to Mom, "Now his back is bothering him, too. I'm going to call Dr. Samuelson."

Doctors cost money so I knew Dad was really worried. I heard him on the phone.

"His foot then his back. Most of the weekend. What about aspirin, ice, heating pad, rest? Doc, he's a kid. Probably strained muscles running around. See him first before sending us on. Okay, let me know when and where." He slammed the phone down.

Pans banged and the kettle whistled. The phone rang again. "Today? So soon? An urgent appointment? Okay, okay. We'll be there." He dialed another number. "Julia, tell the boss I can't come. A family emergency. I'll call back if I won't be in this afternoon. Thanks."

I felt queasy. For Dad to miss work, something must be really, really, wrong with me.

He came back to my room with buttered toast and a glass of milk. He looked tired. "Michael, we have to get to a medical center downtown. Doc Samuelson pulled strings to get you seen by a top man right away."

He helped me dress then carried me down the stairs on his back. All the way, he drove hunched over the steering wheel, his jaw clenched.

I whispered, "Dad, why do we have to rush downtown? Am I going to die?"

Dad shot a glance at me, then slowed the car to normal speed. He said quietly, "Doc said that, sometimes, when boys your age have a growth spurt, bones do not grow evenly. That can cause pain. It's important that you get help as soon as possible so that your body evens out while it is still growing."

Dad didn't tell me then about his cousin Leo, but he saw Leo clearly in his mind's eye. Leo, whom I had never heard, was bent over with a bone deformity that had not been caught in time. Now, he stared down as he walked. That image haunted Dad as he drove into the medical center's parking lot.

He left me in the car and ran into the building, returning with a wheelchair marked UC Med Ctr.

He rolled me down white hallways, into an elevator, then down more hallways until we passed through swinging doors painted with the words: "Pediatric Orthopedics."

There I met Dr. Abrams. He was a big man, even taller than my father, and broader. He had kind blue eyes and a soft voice with an accent. I later learned he had been born in South Africa.

He said calmly, "Hello, Michael. I am sure all this rushing has made you nervous. Your dad got you here quickly because we suddenly had an appointment open this morning. I am going to examine you to see why you feel pain in your back and foot. These people are medical students. Is it okay if they watch as I check you out?"

There were four young men and one young woman crowded into the examination room.

Dad objected, "Doc, I can't have Michael's visit prolonged for you to teach students. I need to get back to work."

"I understand, Mr. Friedman, but we cannot rush our work with Michael, with or without students watching. You were lucky that Michael felt the pain he did. And lucky to get to see us today without the usual wait. A few hours now will spare him much future pain. And by having these students watch, future boys like Michael might benefit."

Dad stopped arguing. He told me later that cousin Leo flashed through his mind again.

A nurse helped me undress down to my boxers. Then, in front of everyone, Dr. Abrams had me try to touch my toes. He pointed out the curve in my spine, how it was evident when they looked at me from the side when I was bent over but not when I stood up. A medical student measured me from my shoulders to my hips, around my chest under my arms and from my spine around to my chest on both sides.

Then I was put back in the chair and wheeled to a room marked "Radiology." The technician had me stand as he wrapped a heavy belt around my waist with a panel that dangled between my legs. He loaded a metal and glass slide into the machine, then told me to hold my breath as he hid behind a wall.

I heard a click. He pulled the metal and glass plate out and loaded another one. I turned at his command so that each of my sides and my back faced the machine. Each time he loaded a new plate and hid behind a wall, I held my breath and heard the click.

He announced that he was going to develop the pictures and bring them to Dr. Abrams. I was wheeled back to the room where Dad waited.

After what seemed like hours (Dad said it was only 45 minutes), Dr. Abrams returned with the students. He turned clipped black and white images onto a light box. "These are X-rays of Michael's spine. They confirm Scheuermann's Disease, which is caused by the bones of his spine growing unevenly. See how these vertebrae are triangular instead of rectangular?

"Michael is a physically active young man going through a growth spurt, the most common profile of a patient with Scheuermann's. The fronts of his vertebrae are growing faster than the backs. He has developed unevenness in his shoulders and a hump in his back that is visible when he bends over.

"He is lucky that the pain came on as early and as acutely as it did, alerting you, Mr. Friedman, that Michael needed to be seen. You are fortunate, too, that Doctor Samuelson immediately referred you to us. I have seen older teens and adults with this disease who were plagued for years with back pain but never suffered enough to see a specialist. By the time they were seen, their bones had hardened and the damage was done. At that point, only extensive back surgery can help but not always to a satisfactory level."

"What can you do for Michael?" Dad asked, his voice gluey with worry.

"We can't cure Scheuermann's Disease but we can limit its impact. We must encourage the spine to grow straighter. We do that with a body cast and weight exercises. Within a few months we will see if the treatment is effective. Surgery can be a later option if the body cast is not successful."

Dr. Abrams put a hand on my shoulder, saying gently, "The treatment is not pleasant, Michael. You will have to wear the cast day and night. You must be brave and patient. But the good news is that, in almost all cases of young men like yourself, the results are excellent. The spine becomes straight enough so the curvature is not visible to the untrained eye and the patient maintains full mobility and flexibility." He waited to see if I had any questions.

I had only one. "Will I be able to play baseball next spring?"

He smiled. "That's an important question. I can't be absolutely certain, but I can say, if you follow all our advice, most probably, yes!"

That had to be good enough.

CHAPTER FIFTEEN

I soon found out that Doc Abrams had not told me the whole truth. The treatment wasn't just "unpleasant." It was downright horrible.

To make the body cast fit right, I was wrapped in plastic film then bandages soaked in plaster of paris were coiled around me from my armpits to my groin. I had to stand still until the whole thing hardened. The techs knocked on my chest and my back until they heard the right sound. Then they cut the mold off and took it away.

Dr. Abrams explained that the plaster cast was shaped as my back was now but the cast that I would wear would be closer to how my back should be, forcing it to grow the right way. It would be uncomfortable at first, but, as my back straightened, it would feel better.

That was the signal that it was time for me to get a new cast to keep forcing my spine into a straighter shape. Feeling comfortable was both good and bad: the old cast had done its job but it was time to be fitted with a new one. Over and over, until my spine was as normal as possible.

What he didn't tell me was that the cast would smell like rotten eggs and that the smell would get worse as I sweated. It also would make me itch. I discovered all that over the next few days.

When we got home, Mom's hands flew up to her mouth in shock. "Oh, my poor boy, what have they done to you?" she moaned.

Dad said sternly, "That is not helpful, Evie. This cast will straighten Michael's spine. He will have to wear it all the time, for weeks, possibly months. It is very important he does that so he will never be like my cousin Leo."

Finally, he told us all about Leo and how his spine was permanently bent so the man could never stand up straight. I got to know this cousin Leo well over the next few months. When I wanted to give up, begging Dad to cut off the body cast regardless of what it might mean to my future, he recited the story of cousin Leo again.

I grew to hate Leo. I even doubted he existed, thinking that Dad had made him up to scare me. But Zayde told me that Leo was a real person, crippled by the same disease I had, or so he thought since he couldn't remember the name. He called it "Shwarmer's Disease."

Bubbe sighed, "The Arabs eat that. Shwarma."

Zayde ignored her and added, "Leo has the sugar disease too. Poor schlimazel. No luck."

"Diabetes," Bubbe corrected.

"That's what I said," Zayde shot back.

"But he is brilliant," Bubbe went on.

"I was about to say that next if you let me," Zayde grumbled. "A brilliant boy who grew up to be a brilliant doctor, a rich doctor who lives in a tall building in Chicago."

Bubbe added, "A big man! With a big practice."

"Not such a big man," Zayde replied. "He walks like a crab so he is not such a big man."

"I meant he only sees people with big problems. For them, he is a big man," Bubbe said firmly.

Zayde rolled his eyes at me. He held up the jar of big sour balls. I picked out my favorite flavor, hoping its sour citrusy taste would distract me from the itchiness of the body cast. And its stink.

My grandparents didn't say anything about the odor which got more pronounced as time went on because I couldn't take a real shower. At the next visit, Bubbe gave me powder, saying, "This will help with itching. It has a nice scent."

My face grew hot. She meant to be kind but, she had confirmed that I smelled. It didn't help that the plastic shaker had a picture of a baby and that it said, in pastel letters, "soothing for baby's delicate skin."

I was grateful for it later when I shook some powder down the front and back of the cast. It reduced the friction against my skin and it disguised the smell…only a little for a little while.

Dad and I argued about school. I told him there was no way I would let the kids see me in the cast. I demanded that he tell the school I had an infectious disease like polio.

Dad was firm. "Michael, truant officers will come to see why you're not at school. They will know that you do not have measles or mumps or anything that spreads. They will make us pay a fine and, in the end, you will be back in school.

"You'll have to tough it out. I will take you the first day to explain 'your situation.'"

Great! Another "situation" in the unlucky Friedman family!

I screamed, "I won't go to the goddamn school and be the goddamn laughingstock! You can wallop me with your belt but I won't go."

Dad yelled back, "Dammit, Michael. You must go. Like I must work to pay all these goddamn bills. For your mother and now for you."

It was a stand-off.

I waddled to my room, slammed the door as hard as I could then leaned against it and cried. I didn't care if only babies cried like that. I didn't care that Karen was on the other side of the flimsy partition hearing me. I didn't care if Dad beat me for cursing and crying and arguing. I just wanted to die then and there.

I heard Dad pacing back and forth in the kitchen, muttering. Then he made a phone call. I couldn't hear what he was saying because I was gasping for air from crying. Then he left.

I sat at my desk. There, among all the pens and pencils in a big jelly jar, was a pair of scissors. I thought, *I'll cut myself out of this thing. I don't care if I grow up to be a crab like goddamn cousin Leo.*

I worked at the top of the cast with the scissors for several minutes, hardly making a dent in it. I threw the scissors against the wall.

I fumed. And itched. I picked up a wooden ruler from my desk and worked it down the back of the cast, using it to scratch the itchy spots. I thought, *What a family. Mom with her Gaucher's and her craziness. And now me with my twisted back. Why the hell were we cursed like this?"*

I spent time idly turning the pages of old comic books and feeling miserable. I got lonely so I went to my mother to see how she was doing. The two Friedman sickies stuck at home together.

She was sitting in bed. When I walked in, she looked up from all the papers strewn about. "Michael, what are you wearing?"

I couldn't be patient. "Mom, you never remember anything! Dad told you. I have a disease that runs in our family. Dad's cousin Leo has it too. My back is crooked. We went to a specialist who charged a lot of money to put this goddamn thing on me. I hate it. It stinks and it itches."

Her mouth formed an "O" and she shook her head. "Michael, why did this happen?"

I felt like throwing all her papers on the floor. She paid attention to them but never to me. I had hoped she would sympathize. I was a goddamn fool!

I heard the apartment door open. It was early for Dad to be home. He called, "Michael, come out here."

I thought, "No!" but I didn't dare say it out loud because that would make him angry. If Dad got real angry, he might take off his belt and beat me, forgetting how expensive the cast was.

I heard more voices. "Come on, Mikey." It was JimmyJoe. My guts shrank into a ball. "Come on out. We have new comics and some Topps packs we haven't opened yet. Mom sent over cookies."

I wiped my face with my hand and cautiously opened the door. I walked out and waited for the twins' reactions.

"Geezus," Joey said, coming closer. "That is the biggest cast I ever seen. Even bigger than Junior's when he broke his leg playing football." He tapped on the top of the cast where it showed under the open collar of my shirt. "Rock hard!" he exclaimed.

Jimmy tapped the cast too. "Solid. Like a rock." He grinned. "Our uncle Rocco is one tough guy. You're sort of Rocco Junior. We'll call you Rocky."

I mumbled, "It smells and it itches."

Joey shrugged. "It's not forever," he said. "Ma said you need to wear it just a few months. It's not like Sam's brace. A forever thing."

Mrs. G knew? I felt better. I was not alone in my misery and I would never look like cousin Leo. And I would not be imprisoned for the rest of my life, like Sam.

I suddenly wanted to see Sam. He would really understand. He would listen to me and help me be brave.

As if he could read my thoughts, Dad said, "Sam will be over later. He stopped by your school to pick up your books and homework. You need to catch up this week so that you are ready to go back on Monday." He said sternly, "You can have this week off to adjust to the cast. I arranged that with the principal. Next week, you go back to school. No arguing! Agreed?"

Next week seemed a long way off. Lots might happen between now and then. My back could straighten up faster than Dr. Abrams ever saw. Miracles happen after all. Perhaps the Friedmans would have some *mazal*, some luck, for a change.

CHAPTER SIXTEEN

There was no miracle.

Every day, Sam brought me my assignments. He did his homework at our house in between helping me with mine. The twins came over a few times each week with their books, too. Mrs. G had told them to get help from Sam, a top student.

When the twins weren't there, I asked Sam how he ignored the stares and comments. He smiled a bit. "I'm lucky in a way. Everyone knows someone who had polio. They know why I limp."

I never thought he was lucky having had polio but I knew what he meant. I had seen Life Magazine's pictures of kids who had polio and had to live in iron lungs, big machines that compressed their chests so they could breathe. Only their heads stuck out and they had to use mirrors to see people near them.

In comparison, Sam was lucky. He could walk and swim and even play some sports...not well, but still he played. And, as he said, people understood what had happened to him.

But Scheuermann's? Who the hell had ever heard of it? And my cast really smelled. I hoped Monday would never come.

But, of course, it did.

On Monday, the weather was cool. After shaking baby powder inside the cast, I pulled a sweatshirt over it, hoping it would hide it. I just looked like a big box with legs.

Dad had made some improvements to the cast. Its edges had chafed my groin, my shoulders and my neck. Ordering me to stand still, he spent a long time filing the edges to smooth them out. He then put heavy tape over them. Not a perfect solution, but I felt good about the time he took to take care of me.

JimmyJoe called on me to walk to school. Some kids from their block were with them, all going a longer way around. They greeted me with "Hey, there, Rocky!" Some guys reached over to tap me on the chest or back.

Joey boasted, "We told them that you were tough like our cousin Rocco. They wanted to see the cast because it sounded so cool."

A kid, called Flash because he was a quick running back on the football team, said, "I want to get me one of those. Won't the defensive ends be shocked when they try to stop me?!""

That raised laughs all around.

At the next corner, Eddie Cohen, the "poor little rich kid," caught up with us. He tapped my cast when Joey told him that I was now 'Rocky.'

Eddie suggested, "You could be a superhero in the comics. Concrete Man, hard as rock. Bullets just bounce off his chest."

Other kids added details about my supe adventures. When we entered the school kids swirled around, wanting to tap my chest or back. I had become a celebrity. The rock-solid kid. Also, the kid with the distinct odor but nobody made much about it.

I was lucky that the days were getting cooler so I didn't sweat. Baseball season was still months away. I hoped I could play by the spring.

When we went back to Dr. Abrams two months later, he cut off the cast then he made the same measurements. He had some good news and some bad news for us.

The good news was that my spine appeared much straighter...not straight but straighter. The bad news was that I still needed a cast. "But," he added, "Michael could try a different type, one that has straps and buckles and could be removed for brief periods. For example, if he wanted to take a bath or shower. However," he eyed my father, "that device costs more since it must be made in a custom shop. And every few months, a new one must be ordered."

Dad had told me that whenever anyone used words like "device" or "specialist," the bills were bigger. Now he clenched his jaw.

Dr. Abrams added in a quieter voice, "We could continue with plaster casts. It is the tried and true technique and much less costly. The results for Michael will be the same."

I thought, *No, it won't be the same. I would smell and itch and have to wear the cast every minute of every day.*

The new cast sounded like real freedom, but I couldn't make the decision. Not when it was for something that was "costly."

Dad finally spoke. "The new kind."

I went through more measurements then, to my surprise, the technicians wrapped me up to make a mold for a new plaster cast, just like the one I hated. I nearly bolted when I saw them lay out the materials.

Dad explained, "The new device will take a few weeks to be made, Michael. For those weeks, you must continue with the old style one. You have come far. We don't want your spine to begin to curve again."

We made an appointment for three weeks later to return for the new device. I planned to mark off the days on the kitchen calendar.

As we left, the nurse handed my dad a paper. "Mr. Friedman, this is the bill for the custom device. It must be paid at Michael's appointment."

My father scanned the bill. His jaw clenched again. He said nothing as we walked to our car. When we drove away, Dad turned in a different direction. I didn't ask him where we were going because I could tell by how tight his jaw was that he wasn't in a talking mood. After a few more turns, though, I realized that we were on our way to Mom's parents, the Schneiders.

When we pulled up in front of their house, Dad spoke for the first time during the trip. "You are coming in with me, Michael. Don't say anything, no matter how loud it gets."

I was surprised by that because Papa and Nanny Schneider were always so quiet when Dad dropped us off for a visit. It was Dad who cursed all the way home after he picked us up.

Nanny answered the bell. She stared in surprise at Dad, then smiled at me, opening the door wider. "How nice to see you, Michael. Come in. You have grown so much since... but what is that you are wearing?"

Dad interrupted her. "This isn't a social call, Minna. Is Reuben home?"

She hesitated then said, "Why, yes, he is."

"Ask him to join us. We need to talk."

We waited in the living room. Its fancy sofa and chairs were covered with plastic that made crinkly noises when you sat down. If you were wearing shorts, you had to get up slowly, peeling your skin away from the covers. When Mom, Karen and I visited, we usually sat in the kitchen where Nanny served cakes out of white boxes tied with string, like Mrs. G got at the bakery.

Soon Papa Reuben appeared. Dad began in a steady, quiet voice, "Reuben, times have been hard for us. You of course know all about Evie's illnesses. She recently landed back in the hospital.

"See this cast Michael is wearing. His spine was growing crookedly so we had to see a specialist for this cast to straighten it. Now he needs a more expensive model for now and new ones over the years...for a long time."

Nanny's hands went up to her mouth, as she shook her head back and forth, muttering, "Oh, oh, oh," softly.

Papa Reuben kept his eyes on me, not looking at Dad. "A man must do what he needs to do for his family."

"Damn it, Reuben. I am doing all one man can do. I work two jobs and I plan to take on more hours, but the kids need me, too. Evie can't help."

"She is a very sick woman," Nanny said sadly.

"Yes, she is a very sick woman. You knew she was sick but you never told me. You were glad I took her off your hands so you didn't have to pay her doctor bills anymore."

Papa Reuben snarled, "You are disgusting, talking that way about your wife, the woman you said you loved when you asked me for her hand.

You couldn't marry her fast enough. Talking that way in front of Michael. Disgusting!"

"My wife, yes! Your daughter still! Sick her whole life. You never said anything to me about her medical crises and her mental wanderings and the problems she would have taking care of children, a home, a husband, about how hard it would be for her to be a wife and mother."

Dad's face was red, but he tried a reasonable tone. "What would you say if a man sold you a car and never told you it had problems? If you needed it to get to work but suddenly discovered that its guts were in bad shape? If that man was honorable, he would help you get the car up and running. Or was he nothing more than a cheat? Glad to get damaged goods off his hands by cheating a poor sucker?"

Reuben looked at Dad as if he was the one who smelled bad. "You compare your wife to a second-hand car? People are not machines. Life is not predictable. No one is guaranteed to never have problems. They just deal with them. A real man takes care of his family."

My father exploded. "I *am* taking care of my family. I am just asking for help from my wife's family. I am asking you to help me care for your daughter. To help me with the bills for her treatments. I will be able to take care of Michael if you do your share for Evelyn."

Papa Reuben shook his head. "I am retired. Money is tight. We barely manage ourselves."

My father waved at the living room furniture. "Barely managing? This suite arrived last year, right? And not from a secondhand store. And the new TV? That came a few months ago. Michael told me when it arrived. Isn't the car in the alley this year's model?" He stopped suddenly. "Forget it, Reuben. Pretend I never came to ask for help."

He turned away then turned back. "This goes both ways, Reuben. If I am working more hours, I won't have time to bring Evie and the kids for visits. I will be too busy earning the money I need to be a *real man*, to take care of my family without any help." He walked out the door.

Nanny gasped and shot a horrified look at Papa Reuben then wrapped her arms around me. "I am so sorry, Michael, that you heard all that. I am so sorry about your back, tateleh. You will still visit, yes?"

I shook my head 'no' and followed Dad out.

We rode home in total silence. Dad smoked cigarettes all the way, something he never did since he didn't like the smell in his car. He stopped in front of the Giudice house.

"Michael," he said, looking worn out, "call on the twins. See if you can spend a few hours here. I need time to think."

"Dad, I am sorry about my back. I'll wear the cheaper cast if that helps."

He rubbed my head. "No, Michael. You are innocent in all this. I won't save money on your health, no matter what else I have to do."

"I can get a job to help out. A paper route? Maybe Sam can get me in with Mr. Finkelman. I can work there a few hours a week for money to help with the bills."

"No. You deserve time to just be a kid." He pounded the steering wheel. "I should have known that shmuck would never part with a dime. Dammit!" His eyes glistened.

That scared me more than anything, more than cursing and threats and even his belt. That Dad was so worn down that he almost cried.

I stumbled out of the car and went up the stoop. Mrs. G opened the door, looked at me then looked at Dad in the car. She put a hand on my shoulder, "Michael, the twins are out back. I'll bring snacks out in a moment."

As I went down the hall to the back door, she kept looking at Dad in the car. Then she went down the stoop towards it. "Dave, let's talk."

I didn't go through the house to the backyard to join the twins. Instead, I went to the living room window. I could see the street from there, so I watched Mrs. G get into the front passenger seat of Dad's car. She talked as Dad shook his head back and forth then leaned it on the steering wheel.

When Mrs. G climbed up the stoop, I scurried to the backyard. The twins were playing Pinners but I didn't feel like playing so I became the umpire. They had to keep on reminding me to pay attention.

A week later, Dad brought the mail into the kitchen where the twins, Sam and I were sitting around the table. Even though I was back in school, we had gotten into the habit of doing homework together.

Mrs. G still wanted Sam to tutor JimmyJoe. In fact, she gave him ten dollars a week to review their work and prepare them for tests. Also, the weather was getting colder and the days were shorter as the harsh Chicago winter approached. By the time our homework was done, it was too dark, windy and cold to play outside.

Even Mom got into the new routine. She would come into the kitchen to make hot chocolate for us. She served it in mugs with a marshmallow bobbing on top. When it melted, it made the drink even sweeter. She would put out a box of cookies and sit on the chair by the phone drinking tea.

No one commented on her color or how quiet she was or that she hummed to herself. The twins were used to the way it was in my house which made it easier on me.

That day, as Dad was going through the mail, we all jumped when he yelped, "What the hell? I don't believe it. The man did the decent thing."

He was staring at a piece of paper in his hand. Normally, he cursed at each paper because it was a bill. He paid only those bills that threatened to cut off service or to start with "collection."

Mom asked, "David, what is it?"

Dad didn't answer her question, instead he said, "Evie, how about you and the kids visiting your folks this Sunday?"

Mom smiled. "That would be nice."

Dad looked at me. I nodded back at him.

Papa Reuben had changed his mind and sent Dad a check. He must have finally realized family members had to help each other.

Dad laughed out loud after he parked in front of Papa Reuben's house that Sunday. There, on the small front lawn, was a sign:

AAA Sewer Repairs.
Excellent work.
Prices you can't beat.

CHAPTER SEVENTEEN

When Dad and I went back to see Dr. Abrams three weeks later, there was good news and then, more good news. My back was straighter and I was taller. Doc said it was the result of a growth spurt and the help I had gotten from the cast.

The more good news was the new removable "device." As the technician put it on me, Dr. Abrams explained how the buckles and straps had to be very tight because loose straps would not have any benefit. He said seriously, looking me straight in the eyes, "Michael, the more hours you wear this appliance, the greater its benefit. So, even though it is removable, leave it on most of the time, even in bed. It can come off only for special times, like going to a party. Two hours tops on any one day. Eight hours tops per week."

"Special times like playing baseball?" I asked.

Dr. Abrams asked how many hours a week I practiced and how long the games were.

Dad answered. "The season won't start for months. I can tell the coaches to limit Michael's practice time. I am usually there so I will help him into the device at the end of practice. We can work it out so that the cast is off eight hours a week or less."

Dr. Abrams responded, "Michael, when you come back for your next visit, I will know if you are following the rules. If you are wearing the appliance enough hours, there will be continued improvement." He patted my shoulder. "You have been a good patient. I know this has not been easy but you are really on the way now."

Dad was as happy as I was. He whistled as he drove home so I felt I could ask, "Dad, you paid the bill in full?"

He nodded.

"But this new cast was very expensive."

He chuckled. "'Appliance,' Michael! When they charge so much, they give it a fancy name." Then he got serious. "I got a raise at Veriflex, not a big one and it was long overdue. And Greenbaum promised me more hours for the weeks before the baseball season starts.

I loved that Dad didn't want to work extra hours once the season started. That made me more daring. "Papa Reuben needed his sewers worked on? How could he afford that and have money for Mom's bills?"

Dad laughed out loud. "Your grandfather has more money than he lets on. Even so, I don't think AAA Sewer Repairs is charging him much. As the sign says, you can't beat their prices!" He added, "Mrs. G is a really good person."

There was even more good news. I was able to take my first real shower in months.

Life fell into a happy routine during the winter despite the Chicago weather with its winds that cut like knives. Since the weather was too cold to play catch, I spent time indoors, wearing the cast most days and nights. The twins and Sam came over several times a week to do homework and my mid-year grades showed the result. They were the highest they had ever been.

I now had to go to Hebrew school more often to prepare for my Bar Mitzvah, less than two years away. Before Dad could complain that it cost too much money, Zayde announced that it would be his honor to pay the tuition. He also said that he would practice "davening" with me whenever I visited.

Bubbe claimed she knew more Jewish things than he did so she would practice with me too.

Zayde scoffed, "When were you a Bar Mitzvah, can I ask?"

Bubbe answered, "With three brothers, I heard the chants for years. Even in my sleep." She sang out with her hands on her hips and her chin in the air, "Bar'chu et Adonai ham'vorach...."

When I laughed, they laughed too. Then Zayde took out his sour balls and we watched the fights on TV. Bubbe clucked at the sight of "two meshuggenahs beating each other to death while the crowd cheered."

I was real busy. Tuesdays and Thursdays after regular school I trudged over to Hebrew School at the synagogue that we joined after Dad had a fight with the one near The Church. On Wednesdays, I helped Mrs. G do her shopping. She still paid me even if her shopping was light. On Mondays, Karen had a school club meeting so I was on Mom duty until Dad got home.

Karen or I had to be home before Dad left for his second job to dose out Mom's pills at night. If Mom felt up to it, she cooked simple meals: hot dogs and baked beans or canned cream of tomato soup with grilled cheese sandwiches. If she felt really well, she made salmon patties which I hated but I ate anyway. I wanted her to know I appreciated that she had cooked for us.

Afterwards, Karen cleared the table, Mom did the dishes and I dried them. We tried to make conversation. Sometimes we really talked together about school and what we did with friends. Other times, we spoke and she nodded but didn't say a word or ask a question. Later, she sat at the table with her papers or went to bed.

Since I was busy after school, Sam came over after dinner to tutor me. The twins came a few times each week to work with us. If we finished before they had to head home, we played cards.

Sam won most of the time. He remembered each card discarded and, if we played poker, he could tell when we were lying about our hands. I told him that he should go to Vegas to win big at the casinos.

He shook his head. "Nah, that's too risky. I plan to go to college to be an accountant like my Dad. That way, I won't be always looking over my shoulder, worrying about the mob."

The twins grew quiet, studying their cards.

Sam added quickly, "Mobsters like Bugsy Siegel and Meyer Lansky. Jewish ones who built Las Vegas."

JimmyJoe muttered something about having to get home. When they left, Sam shuffled the cards as he said sadly, "I didn't mean to make them feel bad. I had forgotten about their dad."

"Their dad? Mr. G?"

He was surprised at my surprise. "I thought you knew about Mr. G's business."

"AAA Sewer Repairs?"

"Not that one. The other businesses that he can't advertise on the side of his truck."

"What do you mean?"

"My dad does the books for restaurants and bars and he knows about payments to the Chicago

Outfit. Sometimes he sees the AAA Sewer Repair truck around the Italian restaurants on Taylor Street."

He added quietly, "The twins are good guys and Mrs. G is a nice lady. I know she wants the boys to be with us as much as possible and to do well in school. We're good for them."

I looked around our drab apartment. How sad it often seemed with Dad working so many hours and Mom holed up in her room, dreaming the days away. I escaped from here to the Giudices'—a house filled with kids' noise, laughter and warm kitchen smells.

Then I remembered how dark it became when Mr. G was home. How the kids got quiet, how they scrunched down over their plates or found reasons to leave the room. Did the twins come over to my home to escape theirs?

Later, when I went to my room, I pulled out the comic books Eddie Cohen had lent me. I looked at issues of the Spectre and the Flash. The cities looked a lot like Chicago. All the villains were mob guys who smoked cigars and wore Fedoras pulled down low over their faces. They had dark hair and thick lips and big noses. I wondered, *What did JimmyJoe think when they read these comics?*

CHAPTER EIGHTEEN

In Chicago, as spring approaches, the weather goes crazy. Bright sunshine and warm temps one day, then the next, cold gray skies and strong winds warning of spring snow. That was how my life seemed too.

My next visit to Doc Abrams was like a sunny day because the news was so good. After taking measurements, he said that I didn't need x-rays. He could see my back was improved just by his examination. I was another half-inch taller too!

He had the tech adjust the "appliance" so that it was uncomfortable again. I accepted that because I knew that was how it did its work.

Doc then turned to Dad and said quietly, "At your next appointment three months from now, we will need to fit Michael for a new appliance."

That meant another big bill which was a big gray cloud in our sunny day.

"How long does he need to wear these things?" Dad asked.

"As long as he is growing which for some boys can be into their early twenties," Doc said. "After that, Michael should wear a lighter appliance for hours each day and overnight so his back remains straight. That would be a lifelong commitment."

A few more gray clouds skittered over the bright sky of good news.

Dad asked, "Can we discuss the baseball schedule? It starts in a few weeks."

As Doc and Dad went over the practice and game schedule, my day got brighter and brighter. I would be back on the team with the twins soon. This year I didn't have to try out. I would be one of the old team members who threw the ball to the hopeful kids!

A week later, more good news brightened our days. Dad had been arguing with Mr. Berger, the man who owned our house and two others on our block. Dad called him a *gonif*, which means 'thief' in Yiddish. He complained that Berger kept raising the rents but fixed nothing in the flats. Dad was the one who repaired stuff. If wind whistled through windows, he caulked the cracks shut. When the refrigerator broke down, Dad got it up and running again.

The rent was due to go up again. This time, Dad didn't wait. He called Berger on the phone. "Look, Berger, I know you're planning to raise the rent come April 1. This year, it won't be so easy. The tenants in your three houses have a list of complaints a mile long. Things that should have been repaired and never were. Things that building inspectors might issue fines for if they hear about them." I wondered how he knew all this since Dad never spoke with any of those people and especially not to Connolly downstairs.

He went on. "I have a solution, Berger. Rather than wait for you, I have repaired many things in this rat-trap. I will do the same for all the houses and all the tenants for a fifty percent decrease in my current rent and the promise of no increase for the next five years. You will have happy tenants, well-run buildings and no trouble from the inspectors. That's got to be worth a lot."

He listened for a moment then added, "I have a friend who has a sewer business. AAA Sewers, it's called. He looked at the plumbing in this building. Says it's not up to code. That could cause trouble. Yeah, yeah. I will take care of all the apartments. Even Connelly's, if he lets me into his dump. Send me a letter so I have it in writing."

When he hung up the phone, he grinned. "I will be super for the Berger houses. I can cut back on work hours so I will be free on your baseball days."

The week after Dad got the letter from Berger, he spoke to the families in the three buildings to make a list of their problems. He created a schedule to work on each apartment. He even planned to paint the stairwells and foyers to make each house brighter. The extra paint he could use to paint our kitchen, making it a nicer place to have the twins over for homework and stuff.

The spring winds still blew and the skies over Chicago were gun-metal gray but, for a while, it was warm and bright in our apartment. But Friedman luck doesn't ever last. Just a few weeks later, gray clouds shadowed our lives again.

Over the weeks leading up to the official start of the baseball season, I had secretly stretched out my times of freedom from the back appliance. Instead of arriving at the ball field with it on, I took it off at home and slid it under my bed, just in case Mom saw it and reported to Dad. I then could walk to practice like a regular kid.

After practice, on the days Karen was at her own activities, I was supposed to put the back appliance back on before I hung out with the twins. I didn't. I was only to stay out until Mom needed her next dose. But we guys got busy. We would go to Finkelman's for a soda or just to read the newest comics or we would head to their house to have cookies fresh from the oven. Often, I glanced up at the big cat clock and gasped at the time.

I rushed home, knowing that I had "shirked my responsibilities" as Dad would have said. But nothing bad ever happened.

Mom would be at the kitchen table or in bed, moving her pieces of paper around, writing her poems. Other days, she was peeling potatoes or carrots at the sink, singing along with the radio. I would sigh with relief and head to my room to pull the brace from its hiding place and strap it back on. I would count out pills from the bottles in the medicine cabinet and hand them to her.

I gradually stretched out my luck, coming home later and later. That meant Mom was on her own longer and the back brace was off longer.

Finally, my luck ran out.

I rushed home, later than usual. I was gasping from running upstairs so, when I saw Dad in the apartment, the room went white and spun in front of my eyes. Dad's angry voice reached me as if from far away.

"Michael," he yelled. "Where the hell have you been? And where is your mother?"

I looked around as if I would spot her hiding in a corner. "Mom? She's not here?"

Dad snarled, "No, she isn't and you are late. When did you see her last?"

I went blank. Right after school I had run home, shoved the appliance under my bed, grabbed my glove, then rushed out to join the twins waiting on the sidewalk. Had I seen her? Had I said 'hello'? Shouted 'good-bye' on my way out? Had I given her pills? Or even a thought?

Dad collapsed onto a kitchen chair, scrubbing his face with his hands. "Michael," he sounded scarier trying to be calm, "think! Did you see her when you got home from school?"

"I can't remember, Dad. I don't think so."

"Holy shit!" Dad said. "That could mean more than eight hours since either of us saw her. She could be anywhere by now, doing anything." He looked at the phone on the wall, sighed, got up slowly and dialed. "I need to report a missing person. About eight hours. I know, but she is a sick woman who hasn't taken her medication. She could hurt herself accidentally," he paused, then added more quietly, turning away from me, "or deliberately. Can you search for her?

"So, you are telling me to just hope a sick woman comes home on her own or survives on the streets alone for a full day and night? Okay, let me leave you her name, address and phone number in case you locate her…by accident."

He slammed the phone back on the wall and slumped in the chair, his hands in his lap, his head bowed. When he looked up, his face was gray, his skin deeply wrinkled around his eyes.

"Michael," he said in a flat voice, "we are on our own. The police will not help until tomorrow or until your mother is a victim of a crime or accident. We must look for her ourselves. How the hell can the two of us find her?"

"But we are not only two," I said. "Sam and his parents can help. Zayde and Bubbe and even Papa Reuben and Nanny."

"No!" my father yelled. "This is private family business." His anger revived him.

"But Dad," I dared to say, "you said to Papa Reuben that families are supposed to help each other. Didn't you mean what you said?"

Dad clenched his fists but he didn't make a move to hit me. Instead he said, "You have a big mouth, Michael." He paused then added, "And a good memory too." When he reached towards me, I didn't flinch. I knew he was not going to strike me from the glistening in his eyes.

I added, "And we have more family now."

"What do you mean?"

"The twins and Mrs. G will help, too."

He was about to say "no" so I went on quickly. "Wouldn't you help Mrs. G if she needed it? Like if one of the twins went missing?"

He didn't have time to answer because the phone rang. We both stared at it as if we had never heard it ring before. Dad swallowed hard then picked it up.

"Yes? I'm David Friedman. Who? Yes, Officer. What did she…? Yes, often disoriented. Is she okay? I'll pay. Where? When? I'll be there."

He hung up the phone but left his hand resting on it and stared at the wall.

"Dad?"

"Your mother is okay, Michael. No, that isn't the whole truth. She is not okay but at least not in any danger. She got to the Robert Hall store, where she tried on clothes then left wearing a dress and shoes she hadn't paid for. The guard said the tags were hanging in plain sight so he knew she wasn't a real thief. She couldn't answer his questions. Just kept crying. The police brought her to the emergency room because she wasn't making sense. From her library card, they got her name and address then connected that to my call. I am going to the hospital now."

"I want to go with you, Dad."

"No, Michael. I will ask Mrs. G if you can stay there until I know more."

I had no interest in playing with the twins. Instead I hung out in the kitchen where Mrs. G put me to work shelling walnuts. She hummed as she worked, not asking me any questions.

I squeezed the nutcracker hard, thinking about my mother wandering the streets because I hadn't gotten home on time. Some walnuts wouldn't crack so Mrs. G gave me a meat tenderizer to bang at them. I pounded away as hard as I could.

When I finally finished shelling all the walnuts, I said, "Mrs. G, I am all mixed up."

She had just added the walnuts to the cake batter but stopped mixing it when I spoke. She wiped her hands on her apron and sat down on a chair. Her hands went searching for a cigarette from the pack on the table. "What are you mixed up about, Michael?"

I looked down at my hands. "I am sad that my Mom is too ill to come home. But I am also glad …sort of. When she's home, things are so…."

"Unpredictable?"

"Yes, that's it. I don't know what to expect. And I don't like having to take care of her. Aren't moms supposed to take care of their kids? Like you do? You are home every day so the twins know what to expect. It's never …unpredictable."

Mrs. G lit her cigarette and thought for a moment. "Michael, we can have mixed feelings about the people we love. I am here for the children because, well, because I need to be the steady one. Like your dad is for you."

I thought about that. Dad *was* steady. Even though he worked long hours, he was at most of my games. He made sure Karen and I had dinner every night or a place to stay if he couldn't get home. Sometimes he was tough on me and on Mom, but I could count on him. He was very predictable. So predictable that I knew when he would pull off his belt to "teach me a lesson," which I suddenly realized hadn't happened in a long time.

It was late at night when Dad came to pick me up. Mr. Giudice had been home but had gone out again so it was just the kids and Mrs. G there. This time Dad accepted a cup of coffee and a slice of walnut cake, especially after Mrs. G mentioned I had shelled all the walnuts.

Mrs. G. shooed the twins upstairs to get ready for bed, then she asked, "How is Evie, Dave?"

Dad shook his head slowly as if just doing that was almost too much effort. "They'll keep her for evaluation. Her confusion is beyond Gaucher's. Something else is wrong."

He raised his cup to take a sip. When he put it down, he couldn't find the center of the saucer because his hand was shaking. When it finally settled in the right spot, he added, "She might need to be sent away... institutionalized...."

Mrs. G patted his arm. "Dave, I am so sorry. But she will get the help she needs."

"How can I afford a good place, Rose? If she goes to one of those public nuthouses...?"

"Shush," Mrs. G. cautioned. "Michael...."

Dad glanced at me and swallowed hard.

"Dave, if it is money...."

"No, Rose. I will figure it out. While I do, it would take a load off me if Michael can spend time here, after school and that."

My heart lifted. I knew I should be sad about Mom but to spend more time with the twins in their bright home with Mrs. G in the kitchen....

As I expected, Mrs. G said, "Of course!"

CHAPTER NINETEEN

Mom was away for weeks, so we all had to get into yet another new routine. I am sad to say now that, as life became more predictable, I was much happier.

When I got home from school on game days, I took my back appliance off, changed into my uniform, ate a sandwich and made some for Dad to take to the game. When Dad got home, he changed into the shirt for his second job and packed his bag dinner while I grabbed my glove, jacket and anything else I needed. He put my back brace in the car trunk for later. By then, Sam had walked over and we got into the car.

We drove to the twins' house where other kids were waiting. There Uncle Jim and Dad divvied us up so we could fit into the two cars. Mrs. G. handed out bags of cookies and fruit for after. Then she piled into Uncle Jim's car and our cavalcade moved out.

Our team was much better that year. Uncle Jim's trumpet rang out more often for runs scored. Coach Fiorello tried me in different positions, finally settling me on second base. I had wanted to be catcher like Dad but Doc Abrams said that position might be too hard on my legs and back.

It didn't much matter to me. I got to play a lot that year. I was a good batter, not so much hitting home runs but hitting line drives and those little punk shots that advanced runners and helped us win games. The team knew that I could bunt a ball so it stayed right inside the baseline, making the catcher and pitcher scramble while our guy advanced to second or the guy on third got home. I could line a base hit far enough into mid-field that fielders missed catching it while they hesitated over who had the best play. I got on base even on little bouncers because I was a fast runner.

I had good hands, too: If I caught the ball, I rarely dropped it and I got it out of my glove fast so that we got more outs. The crowd cheered and the trumpet blared out frequently those days.

If Mrs. G was there, I heard her yelling and cheering. More than I could hear Dad. He said he didn't have to cheer loudly because Mrs. G. yelled enough for both of them.

After the game, Dad dropped me at the twins' for dinner and to do homework. Sam came over to tutor us.

We had to work at the kitchen table so we wouldn't goof off. Mrs. G hovered near, smoking her cigarettes and drinking a glass of beer. When we were done, she put out freshly-baked cookies or slices of cake with glasses of cold milk as our reward. She also checked that I had put the appliance back on as soon as I walked through the door so I never could forget about it.

One day, it was raining buckets. Practice was canceled so Dad said I should stay home, wearing the brace, of course. Sam came over when Dad left for his second job, so we got out the books to work. Both of us jumped when the doorbell rang.

"Maybe it's a mistake? Someone hitting the wrong bell?" I said. "We never get visitors."

"A visitor for Connolly?" Sam asked.

"Right!" I said sarcastically. "If we never get visitors, that goes double for Connolly!"

The bell rang again so I looked out of the living room window. Two identical faces with dark hair plastered against their heads looked up.

"The twins?" I called to Sam.

Sam cleared a space at the table. "Maybe they have a math test coming up?" he suggested.

I didn't think so. They didn't have any books. Something was up. They hadn't called up at me or waved or anything. Just looked up.

I ran down to let them in. They were soaked through. Their shoes made squelchy sounds as we trudged past Connolly's door. He stuck his head out and was about to make a comment. Then he saw the twins and his head pulled back like a turtle's into its shell. He closed his door.

When we got into the apartment, Sam asked, "Need some math help?"

JimmyJoe shook their heads and stood there, dripping on the kitchen floor. Finally, Joey spoke up. "Pop's gone."

"Gone?" I repeated.

Jimmy mumbled the word again. "Gone."

Not left town or went away. Just gone.

Sam persisted. "Whaddya mean, 'gone?' Don't you know where he went and why?"

They shook their heads, back and forth in rhythm then shrugged at the same time. Joey said, "No one tells us anything. He's just gone."

"But he doesn't always come home," I said, remembering the times when I slept over and the black car wasn't in the alley all night.

"Ma doesn't cry those times," Jimmy said.

"Her eyes are all red and she is smoking cigarettes, one after the other. And the house is a mess," Joey added.

"There weren't any fresh cookies when we got home," Jimmy whispered.

That was serious.

Sam told me to get towels so the twins could dry off. He put out glasses for milk and shook Oreos out from the bag we had opened. The twins sat down and sipped milk and munched cookies. We didn't talk, just sat in silence for hours.

When we heard Dad coming up the stairs, JimmyJoe looked at each other and said, "We got to get home."

"Tell my dad what you told us. Maybe he knows something."

They shook their heads again. "You know what we know."

They hurried down the stairs, passing Dad on their way. I heard them say, "Hi, Mr. Friedman. Bye, Mr. Friedman," then the door shut loudly behind them.

Connolly's head popped out. "Friedman, there's way too much running on the stairs. Sounds like a damn army marching up and down."

Dad said, "Connolly, close your damn door and mind your own business."

This time, Connolly's door slammed shut.

Sam and I explained what the twins had said. Dad sat down at the table with his raincoat on, his wet hat still on his head. Water was pooling on the floor again but he didn't notice it.

"Gone? That is all they said," he asked.

Sam and I nodded.

"Okay," he said, slapping his hands on his knees. He got up and went to the phone.

"Rose, Dave here. Can you talk? The twins told Michael something about Lou.... Don't cry. I can't understand what you're saying. I'm coming over now. Don't argue. I'm on my way." He hung up then stared into space for a few seconds before asking, "Michael, where's the paper?"

He turned pages, scanning each quickly. He stopped at one marked "Local News."

I asked, "Dad, what is it?"

No answer.

"What is it?" I repeated.

He finally read out loud, "Local Mob Boss Arrested. After several months of investigation, the police raided a known hangout of the Giudice outfit, arresting several men on charges of racketeering. According to the district attorney, the Giudice outfit used a sewer business as a cover for its operations. Luigi Giudice, the owner of AAA Sewer Repairs, is in custody. The D.A.'s office has not answered questions about his whereabouts or his willingness to cooperate. There are unconfirmed rumors that the business had several city contracts which are also being investigated."

Dad shook the paper. "That poor woman." He looked at me. "Michael, I am going over to talk to Rose to see if I can help in any way."

"I want to come with you."

He shook his head. "This is a serious matter. Nothing for kids to get involved in."

"But, Dad, the twins are my friends and they are involved."

Uncle Dave, you should have seen them," Sam added. "They were really messed up. They came here to find help."

"But they left as I got home," Dad said.

"They knew that Michael would get you to help," Sam responded.

Dad sighed. "Okay, Michael, get your books and stuff. You and the boys need to give Mrs. G and me time to talk. Got it? Your job is to keep the twins out of the kitchen while I talk to Mrs. G."

Sam gathered his stuff and headed home. Dad and I got umbrellas and walked across the lot to the twins' block.

The street was very quiet. Not just because of the rain. No one was walking home from work or shopping. No one even looked out of a window. It was as if all the houses had folded up into themselves.

When we knocked at the front door, it was answered by Connie. For once, she looked awful. Her hair was a mess. Her eyes were puffy and her nose was red.

Dad said, "I told your mother I was stopping by."

She held the door open for us. The front of the house was very dim, the drapes drawn closed, shutting out the gray light of the rainy day. Even so, I could see that the living and dining rooms were wrecked. Cushions had been opened, their fillings pulled out. The contents of shelves and cabinets covered the floor. Family photos were lying face down on tables, the backs of the frames ripped open.

Dad muttered, "Oh, God."

He pushed me down the hallway to the kitchen where Mrs. G sat at the table, smoking, the ashtray in front of her filled with stubs. Her face was gray, her eyes red.

She rose, moving towards the coffee pot, but sat down again when Dad said, "Rose, I don't need anything. I just want to talk." He turned to me. "Michael, find the twins and get to work on your homework."

I had no more homework to do but I got his message: keep the twins out of the kitchen. I found JimmyJoe sitting halfway up the stairs. I sat on the step just below them.

"Hey, what's up?" I asked.

Jimmy said, "Junior's gone too."

"Oh" was all I could think of saying. "Oh."

"Goddamn Junior," Joey hissed angrily. "I bet he said something he shouldn't have to someone he shouldn't have. He's so dumb."

From where we sat, the voices in the kitchen were just faraway mutterings. Joey looked at Jimmy and me. "Let's get closer."

We moved down to the bottom step. I pulled comic books from my backpack, the latest shipment from Eddie Cohen. We each opened one and let it lay in our lap so we could grab them to pretend we were reading. Right now, we wanted to listen, but we only heard bits and pieces from the kitchen.

Dad: What happened?

Mrs. G.: mutter, mutter...save Junior.

Dad: mutter, mutter.

Mrs. G.: ...foolish. And...Junior...drugs....

Silence for a few moments.

Dad: mutter, mutter...lawyer say?

Mrs. G.: ...if he cooperates....

Dad: ...family safe?

Mrs. G.: ...Police search...I know nothing. I have enough to get by. But....

Dad: Don't worry.... all family now.

Silence.

Dad: There, there. You helped us. Now we will help....

Again, silence in the kitchen. And on the stairs where we sat.

I whispered, "Don't worry. You heard Dad. We are all family now."

JimmyJoe wiped their eyes. When we heard a chair scrape on the kitchen floor, we raced up the stairs to their room.

CHAPTER TWENTY

For a few days, the twins were very subdued. People around them were quieter too. The ladies on their street stopped talking when we walked past. Even the kids at the corner, waiting to walk to school with us, joked less than usual.

There were embarrassing moments all the time. At Finkelman's, the new comics showed the good guys fighting the bad mob guys who, as usual, wore fedoras and had fat lips and big noses. I had never seen Mr. G in a hat, but I still spun the magazine rack to face the other way. The movie house featured mob movies each week. Weeks went by before we even thought of going to see a film. No one talked about the latest episode of "Dragnet," our favorite TV show. Instead, we stuck to the Westerns.

Later that week, we all went back to the twins' house where Sam met us for math tutoring again. As I walked into the house, I noticed that the living and dining rooms had been cleared up and the drapes were opened to let in the sunshine.

Delicious warm smells met us from the kitchen. Mrs. G smiled when we entered. Even though she was quieter than usual, she looked better. Her hair had been done and she wore lipstick. The ashtray held only one cigarette.

"Good to see you, Michael, Sam," she said as she put glasses of milk in front of us. "No dawdling, boys," she ordered. "Get to work."

During the weeks that followed, the "Giudice Outfit" case was often in the papers. Dad would read out the bits he found. Something about protective custody, guilty pleas, cooperating witnesses. I didn't get all of it but it seemed that Junior would be home soon but not Mr. G.

Still, things began to fall back into place. I don't remember if we won our next game but I was happy hearing Mrs. G's voice above all the others, cheering us on.

Mom had been away for weeks when Dad announced one night that we would all go to visit her on Sunday, the first time for Karen and me.

Dad said, "She is much better, much calmer. The treatments seemed to have worked."

"What treatments?" I asked.

He shook his head. "I won't describe them, Michael. They were not pleasant but the doctors said they have had good results."

I thought I understood. Treatments like my cast, not pleasant but having good results.

But that did nothing to reduce my confused feelings. I was glad Mom was getting better and would be coming home soon, but I worried about how different she would be. I also worried that life wouldn't really be better, that it would soon be chaotic again.

I spoke to Mrs. G. about my feelings on our next shopping trip. She said nothing until she parked the car. "Change is scary, Michael. As much as we might want some things to change, when they do, we aren't sure that the new way is better. That's why people say, 'Better the devil you know than the devil you don't.'"

I must have looked confused because she tried again. "Michael, in your house and in ours, there were things going on we didn't like. We wished they would change. But, as things changed, we felt nervous about our new life. It just takes time to get used to how things are now." She patted my hand. "Here," she said briskly again, "is my list. Read it off to me so I get everything I need."

I was nervous about visiting the "institution," as my Zayde called it when I was over at their apartment. He asked, "How is your mother doing in that institution?"

Bubbe told him, "Shah! Quiet!".

He retorted, "I am only asking" then Bubbe scolded, "*Ton nit fregn dem kind!*"

When she switched to Yiddish, I knew she was warning him not to talk in front of the child, to keep things from me. Naturally it made me more nervous about seeing Mom.

The 'institution' was Chicago State Hospital, a big brick building sitting in an open field. It didn't look so bad as we drove up to it. Then I saw the tall chain-link fence that surrounded it. There was an eerie silence as we entered through the big doors.

A woman at the front desk was talking to a man in uniform, whose belt held a collection of keys along with a small bat made of black rubber. It looked like a smaller version of the nightstick the cops carried. I swallowed hard.

When we approached the desk, the woman smiled as if she was glad to see us. Dad said he had called to arrange for our visit.

As she wrote out a pass, the man shook Dad's hand. "I'll take you to see Mrs. Friedman. Your missus is in the Rec Room."

We followed him down hallways smelling of disinfectant, just like the ones in the hospital where I went for my back casts. But here, every few yards, there was a door that the guard had to unlock with a key from the bunch on his belt. We saw only a few people.

Dad explained, "This floor has public rooms, recreation areas, dining rooms and offices. The treatment rooms are in a different wing. The patients' rooms are upstairs. On the weekends, it's pretty quiet. Fewer treatments and more visitors. Like us."

We turned into a big room where people sat around tables, busying themselves with projects. In the corners, small groups were talking quietly. Families, I guessed, like ours, coming for a visit.

At one table, four women sat knitting. A black woman in a bright smock moved around, helping them. They all looked up as we approached.

It took a few seconds before Mom recognized us, then her face lit up. She looked pretty. Her shiny hair was brushed into a ponytail and her lips were bright with lipstick. She wore a normal green and white dress, instead of the hospital gown I had expected. I let out my breath.

"Evelyn," the black woman said, "your family has come to visit. Your husband…." She paused.

Mom said nothing so Dad filled in the pause. "David."

"And your daughter," the woman continued.

"Karen," my dad said.

"And your son," the woman went on.

I couldn't stand it. I blurted out, "Mom, it's me, Michael. Don't you recognize me?"

Dad put a hand on my shoulder. "Michael has grown and, with his back straighter now, he looks much taller, doesn't he, Evie?"

My mother's smile grew wider. "You do look different, Michael. And Karen, your hair is different too. It is very becoming."

"Connie Giudice did it, Mom. She is learning to be a beautician. She practices on me."

"Connie?" My mother asked slowly, her gaze going back and forth between the black woman and Dad.

Dad helped her. "Connie is the twins' older sister. You remember JimmyJoe—Michael's best friends."

Mom nodded slowly, then she looked down at her hands, still holding knitting needles. "I am knitting you a scarf, Dave," she said. "It is blue. Your favorite color."

I didn't know Dad had a favorite color. It must've been blue because he smiled. "Great! I can really use it come winter."

The black woman said, "My name is Grace. I have been teaching Evelyn to knit. She is doing very well." She helped Mom to her feet. "Come, Evelyn. You and your family will be more comfortable near the windows."

She settled Mom into a chair then motioned us to pull chairs closer so we could talk quietly, like the other families. She leaned over to Dad and said, "Doctor Schulein is in and would like to have a word with you all." Then she asked, "Would you all like something to drink? Some pop for you kids and perhaps coffee for you two?" She looked at Mom and Dad as if they were seated in a restaurant and she was taking their order. Dad nodded and she bustled away.

Silence hung over us for a few moments, then I blurted, "Are you coming home soon, Mom?"

Mom looked at Dad. "Am I going home soon, David?"

Dad spoke cheerfully. "You will come home soon, Evie, if you continue to get better. You must work hard to make them see you are better. Show interest in what they ask you to do."

She stared at him as if she was putting his words into a language she understood. I thought of all the times she had seemed to be a visitor from another planet. I sighed.

Dad must have heard me. He changed the subject. "The kids' report cards have been great. Karen has straight As and Michael has gotten great marks too. Bs in math and science! Sam has been tutoring him and the twins."

For the first time Mom put her knitting down. She held out her arms and hugged Karen then me. "I am so proud of you." Then she asked, "Sam?" Heavy silence landed on us again.

We hadn't heard any footsteps but suddenly a man was there, standing behind Mom, smiling at us. He held out his hand to Dad. "I'm Doctor William Schulein. I've been supervising Evelyn's treatments. I want to discuss how she's doing."

As he sat, Grace returned with a tray of drinks and several packets of cookies, putting them down on a table nearby and inviting Karen and me to move over, away from the adults. But my eavesdropping ability had gotten better, I guess, because, as I munched, I heard a lot of what the doctor said.

He began by saying to Mom, "Evelyn, I am going to bring David up-to-date with how you are doing. Is that okay?" After she nodded, he continued, "We are pleased with the results of the ECT." Dad looked puzzled so the doctor explained, "The treatment we discussed before. Electroconvulsive therapy or, as some people used to call them, shock treatments. Now we refer to the treatments as ECT for short." Dad shot a quick glance at Karen and me.

I made like my snack was extraordinarily interesting, but my mind had stopped at the words "shock treatments." It was flooded with images of the monster, tied to the table, shrieking and twisting as Dr. Frankenstein pulled the switch. Was that what the doctor meant?

I focused back on what he was saying. "The therapy was successful at stopping repetitive ways of thinking and behaving. She is better able to take care of herself as well as to learn new skills such as knitting, as you see.

"Unfortunately, there are side effects with ECT. Memory loss and confusion are common. She has a bit of aphasia—difficulty in saying or writing the right words in the right sequence, but, from the papers you showed me, she had some form of aphasia previously. Our therapists will continue to work with her after she is discharged. We expect that over the next few months her memory and speech will become normal, but she could relapse into old behaviors. We need to discourage that.

"We want her to participate more actively in family life. She will be aided by schedules for certain activities, such as days for cleaning and doing laundry and by having women in to help her do those tasks. Keep items away that might trigger old compulsive behaviors. And, for a while, have someone accompany her on outside errands to keep her focused on the tasks at hand.

"We are also trying new medications. One of them, Miltown, has become widely used for anxiety. Patients have had remarkable results."

Dad shook his head. "I don't want her doped up. Her problem was understanding real life. She was often lost in a dream world."

Again, my mind flashed with images from movies. Stumbling drunks and drug addicts. Like in *The Man with the Golden Arm.*

The doctor held up a hand to halt Dad's words. "That is what is so good about this new medication. It alleviates anxiety without inducing a drugged haze. It is used safely by millions."

Mom was looking at Dad. She seemed to not be listening then she asked, "Am I going home soon, Dave?"

Dad looked at her and took her hand. "Yes, Evie. Soon. You will be coming home real soon."

The doctor nodded, "Yes, Evelyn, you will go home to your family very soon. In fact, I am planning to discharge you next weekend. Then, all of you will be together to begin a new life."

CHAPTER TWENTY-ONE

Every day, during the next week, when Karen and I got home from school, someone came to the house to do something. First, Mrs. G and Connie arrived in Mrs. G's big car loaded with mops, brooms, pails and bags of cleaning stuff. A Hispanic woman, Olga, came with them.

"Olga helps me each week," Mrs. G said. "This week, she will help here so that everything is ready for your mother's return."

As Olga set to work in the kitchen, Mrs. G ordered Karen and me into the bedroom. "Go through all your clothes, toys and books. There must be things you don't use anymore, clothes you grew out of, toys you are too old for. You should make space for new things. Put the old stuff in these bags and we will bring them to The Church for children who need them. Connie, you help Karen and I will help Michael."

As we worked, Mrs. G held shirts and pants up against me and made piles: a "too small" pile, a "too worn" pile, a "to be mended" pile and the pile of "still good." She never mentioned that she had given me most of the "still good" clothes.

Before anything was put back, Mrs. G lined the drawers with cedar paper. She explained that would keep the moths and silverfish away and make the clothes smell nice.

She asked me to leave out the "to be mended" pile but to put the worn and small clothes into a bag and put it into the car to be delivered at The Church. For the first time, I had a bag of things to give to someone else who needed them more!

When I returned, she had stripped our beds down to the mattresses and taken the curtains off the window on Karen's side. She sent Connie and Karen down to the laundry room in the basement to wash and dry the bedding with all the laundry.

When the twins arrived, they were sent to lug an ironing board and iron from the trunk of the car. As Olga set up the board to iron the washed laundry, Mrs. G told the twins to help me sort through my toys and books. I didn't have many toys so we went through them quickly. Mrs. G had given me a rule: if I hadn't played with a toy in the last year, I should put it in a box for Olga's little boys.

Then we started going through the comic books. That took longer because we began reading them and pointing out good jokes to each other. Mrs. G came back when we laughed too loudly. She stood at the door with her hands on her hips and tsked at us. She didn't scold. She didn't have to. Her tsking was enough for us to work faster.

I filled a box with toys to give to Olga for her children and slid two boxes of comics, baseball cards and other stuff back under my bed. But we weren't done yet.

Mrs. G ordered the twins and me to turn the mattresses, something I didn't remember ever doing. As we hoisted them up, Olga ran the vacuum over the box spring then over the new side of the mattress. I didn't even know dust hid in those places.

When Dad got home, Mrs. G, Olga and the twins were gone, but the evidence of their work was all around. The apartment smelled lemony fresh and the curtains on the windows were clean, crisp and ironed.

Dad muttered, "I should have finished painting before Rose did all this work."

Karen said, "Mom will love the new cream paint in the bedroom and the bathroom, Dad."

He picked up a note left on the kitchen table and started to laugh. "She's some lady, Mrs. G. She said just what you said, Karen. 'Your wife will love the cream color in the bedroom and the bathroom. The living room will look lovely in a light blue. Karen and Michael can pick out new colors for their rooms. Put the paint purchase under Giudice at Lichts. You'll get a discount that way.' That's a lot of painting for me to get done in just a few days so let's go, kids."

On Wednesday, I went shopping as usual with Mrs. G. She asked me what my mother enjoyed eating. I tried to think of meals that had gone beyond cans and freezer boxes.

Mrs. G asked questions to help me think. "Does she like pasta? Red sauce? Cheese? Vegetables? Meatballs?" Everything she listed made my mouth water so I nodded. Even if Mom didn't like those things, none of it would go to waste.

On Thursday, Mrs. G returned to our apartment with a trunk full of foil-wrapped packages, each one labeled and with cooking instructions. She put some in our tiny freezer for 'later' and some in the refrigerator for "right away." She looked around with her hands on her hips and a smile on her face, remarking on the fresh paint in the bedrooms.

"It looks wonderful," she said quietly. Then even more quietly, "Evelyn is a lucky woman."

The next day was Friday. In the late afternoon, Bubbe and Zayde arrived with more foil-wrapped packages, a big pot of chicken soup and a roasting pan filled with brisket in gravy.

As Bubbe poked around in the Fridge, she said, "Who's been here? The icebox is full! There is no room for my kugels." She read out labels, mispronouncing the words: "La Sag Knee? Brack Eye Olla? Oh, this I know! Meat balls!"

Zayde added, "That Eye-talian lady must've brought stuff—the one Mikey talks about. With the twin boys. It's all Eyetalian."

I piped up, "Mrs. Giudice!" but I knew they were too busy arguing to even listen.

"Of course," Bubbe answered Zayde with a snort. "An Italian lady would cook Italian. I am sure she is an excellent cook but it's Friday night. On Friday night, we eat Jewish. The Italian food can wait."

Bubbe put her soup pot on the stove with a bang and slid the brisket into the oven to warm. As she bent to set the temperature, Zayde rolled his eyes at me.

"Don't you roll your eyes at me when I talk the truth!" Bubbe said, still facing the oven. "*Fun a nar hot men tsar.*'"

"Hah!" Dad had walked in, the sound of his footsteps lost in the commotion in the kitchen. He was laughing. "'From a fool, one gets grief,'" he translated as he went over to kiss his mother.

"That's the truth!" Bubbe declared as she unfolded a crisply ironed tablecloth to cover the kitchen table. "Now, David, where's the Hoover? Take it out and let Michael give the living room a once over. Where's Karen? She can help me set the table. David, reach up there and get the platters. And you," she turned to Zayde, "here's a cloth.

Dust around the place. Not too hard a job for an *alte man* like you."

Zayde took the cloth and grumbled, *"Mshuge!* The dust comes back as soon as you're done. *Empteyng di okean mit a lefl!"*

"Wait!" I yelled. "I get that! Emptying the ocean? With a…?"

Zayde patted me on the head, "Mit a spoon! Empteyng the ocean mit a spoon. Mickele, you know Jewish! *Ir zent a hel eyngl!"*

"Of course, he is a bright boy! What took you so long to know that!" Bubbe retorted as she motioned Zayde to get to work.

We were all busy and we were all smiling.

When the doorbell rang again, I ran to answer it before Mr. Connolly got angry. Aunt Jennie, Uncle Bernie, Sam and Sherrie were there with big bags from Robert Hall's department store.

As Sam and Sherrie started up the stairs, the big bags thumped on each one, matching their awkward steps. Connolly opened his door, his TV blasting behind him. "For Christ's sake, how many goddamn people do you expect? It is like a goddamn herd going up and down here."

Uncle Bernie listened to the TV noise from Connolly's apartment for a moment. "The Bears are doing really badly, aren't they?"

Connolly scowled, "They stink!"

Uncle Bernie shrugged, "The season's early yet. They might come 'round."

Connolly snorted, "Only Blanders and Brown are worth anything. The others aren't worth shit."

"They score more than the Blackhawks do."

"None of the 'hawks are worth a flying f...."

"That's for sure," Uncle Bernie cut in.

I decided to take a chance. "Mr. Connolly, sorry about the noise but my mom is coming home soon. She's been in Chicago State for weeks. We are trying to get things nice for her."

Connolly looked hard at me. I waited for a nasty comment about Mom being a nut case. He looked up the stairs then back at me. "Tough break, kid. I hope she feels better. She's a nice lady." He shut his door quietly.

"Well, whaddya know?" I whispered.

The big bags contained new spreads for all our beds. Dad tried to pay Uncle Bernie for the things but he shook his head, "I got it covered. Family does for family, Dave."

Sherrie and Karen were already smoothing out her new spread, bright with rainbow stripes. Mine was still in its bag. It had Chicago Cub logos all over it. It was perfect for me but I had a real problem and Sam knew it.

"I can't wait to hear you explain that design to the twins since you said you were such a big White Sox fan." Then he smiled. "Michael, by now, it won't matter at all."

The doorbell rang yet again. When I ran down to answer it, Mr. Connolly's door stayed shut. I could hear him cursing at the TV so I knew he was still alive. Just not interested in us that day.

Standing on the stoop was a delivery man holding a huge basket of flowers. "Friedman?" he said. "Sign here."

I signed but I had no change for a tip. "Wait," I said, taking the basket and climbing back up the stairs.

The basket was so big I couldn't see Dad's reaction but I could hear him. "What the...?" he said as he ripped off the card that was attached. "From Reuben and Minna. 'To our dear daughter. Hoping you get well soon.' Well, it's the least they could do. Here, Michael, give the guy a tip."

As I went back down the stairs, I heard Zayde say, "Such a goyishe thing. To send that instead of food she can eat."

"Food?" Bubbe said, stirring her soup. The smells were snaking down to the front door. "Where would we put more food? Sending flowers shows that at least they thought of her."

Zayde snorted, "It was definitely 'at least' they could do. You can't do more 'at least' than that. Not a hand does that *gonif* raise but to call on the phone and have someone else deliver something. Not even coming theirselves."

"Shush!" Bubbe scolded. *"Di kinder veln hern."*

"So, they hear. You think they don't know the truth of who's their real family?"

Dad called Karen and me into his bedroom. He had painted it a light blue and Aunt Jennie had picked out a spread with lots of blue flowers all over.

"Kids," he said quietly. "When your mother comes home tomorrow, the rest of the family will stay away a few days so she can settle in. I've put all her papers in the basement storage. Doc said it is important that she not return to her old habits. Understand? Don't say anything about her poems or tell her where they are. If she asks about them, try to talk about something else to change her thinking. Got it?"

I got it but it felt that we were ganging up on Mom, keeping secrets from her, forcing her to be a different person. I suddenly missed the papers. That was what Mom loved, all her words on all those papers. I wasn't totally ready to say good-bye to the only mother I knew. I wasn't sure I would like this new woman who still seemed lost somewhere far away.

The next day, when Dad ushered Mom into the apartment, Karen and I both held our breaths, wondering what she would say or do. She looked around as if she had never been there before, then she smiled. She held out her arms and we both ran into them. Of all the things she could have said or done, she first just wanted to hug us.

"Oh, my dears," she said quietly. "I missed you so much." She sniffled, Karen wiped her eyes, I swallowed hard, and Dad cleared his throat.

"Here, Evie, put down your stuff and take a look around," he said.

He took her by the arm and walked her through the apartment, showing off all the new touches. "Do you like the new curtains in the kitchen? Look at the blue color in the bedroom. And the kids' rooms. They picked out their favorite colors. We wanted everything to be fresh and new for your return."

"For a new start," Mom said. "A healthy new start." She was repeating the doctor's words.

"That's right, Evie. A healthy new start," Dad said softly.

CHAPTER TWENTY-TWO

We had a week of quiet days, just the four of us together. But there were caring eyes watching how we were doing. The refrigerator never seemed to have less food. As if by magic, more Jewish and Italian dishes appeared, all wrapped in foil with instructions taped to the top.

When we got home from school, Bubbe and Zayde were there. Bubbe was teaching Mom her recipes. She had brought over an old Danish cookie tin to store the Mandelbrot they made together. Warm dinner smells filled the apartment as we all sat around the table, snacking on babka or cookies or Mom's Mandelbrot.

If the twins called on me for a game of catch, Mom set out glasses of milk for them too and offered her homemade treats from the tin. Then she settled in a chair by the big window in the living room to knit. She smiled, watching us talking with Zayde about the White Sox's pennant win. If someone spoke to her, she would think carefully before answering, then wait to see, by our reactions, if her answer was a good one.

One day, in early October, after school, I opened the front door and found Zayde in the foyer balancing a plate of Mandelbrot resting on top of his jar of sour balls. He had just knocked on Connolly's door. I waited to see what happened.

Connelly cracked the door open, peering out with his eyes narrowed. "Who are you and whaddaya want?" he snarled, but his eyes were on the food.

"I'm Abe Friedman. Got the game on?" Zayde asked. The first game of the World Series between the White Sox and the LA Dodgers was being played in Chicago that afternoon.

"Whaddaya expect? Finally, the Sox get to the World Series! I ain't going to miss an inning. But I thought you guys were Cubs' fans." Another reason he didn't like us.

Zayde sighed. "I have no choice, do I? The Cubs gave me *tsouris* all season. This year, all Chicago got to be Sox fans. I brought some stuff for noshing…. Got any cold beer to go with…?"

The door opened wider. "C'mon in. Got Elson on the radio for the play by play. I won't listen to Scully and Brickhouse. Sticking with the home team all the way."

Zayde saw me watching and winked. "Tatele, if you finish your school work fast, c'mon down to watch the game. You could wait your whole life to see Chicago in the World Series again."

Connelly laughed, a sound I had never heard. "You got it, Friedman. We've had a lifetime of whaddaya call it…."

"Tsouris! That's Jewish for a bellyful of grief."

180

For the first time in my life, I crossed the threshold of Connolly's apartment. Ours had never been as bad. Newspapers and empty beer cans were piled everywhere. No surface was clear except for one window where light poured through crystal objects on glass shelves, creating rainbows that danced on the ceiling and the walls.

Connolly noticed me looking. "My wife," he said quietly, "loved that stuff. Waterford crystal. Irish. I bought her a piece every birthday and anniversary. She's gone now...."

Zayde replied softly, "Women. They complain about dusting tschokes but they love the stuff."

Connolly turned his attention back to the game. "11-0. Whadda game so far! But there are four innings left. The Sox can still blow it...."

"You sure you're not Jewish? Always expecting the worst?"

Connolly laughed for the second time.

Saturday, October 3, was my twelfth birthday. Zayde joked that in my honor the World Series had taken a break. There were no games that day.

To celebrate, Dad took all of us, including Bubbe and Zayde, to see the movie, *Auntie Mame*. I had begged to see something about gangsters or space creatures but Dad said the movie had to appeal to everyone, girls and women included, because, for the first time in a long time, Mom was coming with us.

That settled it. I sat next to Mom and Dad. Karen sat on Dad's other side. We snuck a glance at each other behind our parents' backs when we noticed they were holding hands.

Dad had said we could buy candy from the concession stand as a special treat for my birthday. I got my usual Atomic Fireballs plus Black Taffy, which I loved because it turned my teeth and tongue black. Karen said made me look gross which made me like it more.

Bubbe and Zayde sat in the row in front of us which wasn't a problem since they were short and didn't block our view. As soon as the lights dimmed, Bubbe pulled a crinkly bag from her big black purse. She offered it around, saying, "Instead of that dreck, eat something good."

I loved Bubbe's cookies. They never tasted exactly the same because she added in whatever was in the Fridge or cupboard: a handful of raisins, a chopped-up apple, spoonsful of jelly or the last bit of honey from the Teddy Bear bottle. The cookies were lumpy and hard, but, dipped into milk or hot chocolate, they became a special treat. In the dark theatre, I sucked on a cookie to soften it enough to take a bite.

Zayde, not to be outdone, pulled a bag out of his sports coat pocket. Of course, it was filled with sour balls.

Zayde didn't know how to whisper. "Have one!" he urged us. "One lasts the whole movie."

The usher rushed to our row and shone his flashlight on Zayde. "No snacks from home allowed in the theatre, sir."

"I got the *zucker* disease and all these," Zayde waved his hand at Bubbe's and his bags of treats, "are made *mit no zucker*? I tell you zilch, nadah, none! I could have an attack from eating that stuff you sell. Then whaddya going to do? Go bother someone else."

He waved like the kid was an annoying fly. The usher went to find someone else breaking the rules.

Bubbe said to Zayde, "Keinehora! You are tempting the evil eye! For that, you will get the sugar disease!"

"Bah! I don't believe those Bubbemeisers! Old wives' tales."

"Shush, you two," my father said but he chuckled.

It turned out that the movie was good. Auntie Mame was funny. When her nephew Patrick came to live with her after his father died, she taught him all sorts of crazy things about having a good time.

Zayde kept on calling Mame a *meshuggenah* but laughed so hard at her funny adventures that Bubbe had to pound him on his back when he started to choke.

"No more of those candies," she scolded. "Not when you talk, laugh and eat at the same time!"

Despite laughing at Auntie Mame, Zayde was indignant. "This movie! The Depression wasn't such a laughing stock. It was hard to get work. We Jews had to work on Shabbos if we wanted to keep a job. Remember when I drove a dairy truck and sold milk and bread house to house. I came back with as much as I had loaded on the truck in the morning. No one had money to buy."

"But we had milk and bread for the *kinder*," Bubbe reminded him. "We could give some to the neighbors. They paid you whenever they could."

"Shush," Dad said again, but patted Zayde's shoulder. "No talking now. Just enjoy."

"This meshuggenah lady makes it all a joke. She doesn't know from it," Zayde said, digging another sourball from his bag.

When people shushed Zayde, he offered them sourballs. He whispered to me, "They can't shush at me with sourballs in their mouths."

We were all in the car when Dad smacked his forehead. "I have some things in the trunk that I meant to deliver to Mrs. Giudice. Let's stop there before we go for ice cream."

Zayde smacked his forehead also. "Me too. I was supposed to remind you to remember to deliver that something to the Eyetalian lady."

He elbowed Bubbe in the backseat. She added, "Oh yes, if your head wasn't attached, you'd leave it hanging in the hall closet with your hat."

Dad laughed. "You guys should be on stage."

Bubbe shrugged her shoulders and looked out the window on her side. Zayde looked out the window on his side. I was crowded between them so I could barely shrug at Karen when she turned around to see if I knew what that was all about.

Mom turned in the front passenger seat to look past Karen at Dad. "Did I forget something?" she asked, worry making her voice small.

Dad reached across Karen to pat Mom's knee. "No, Evie. It's my Mom and Dad being my Mom and Dad. They have this comedy routine almost down pat. Confusion and blame all around."

When we got to the Giudices' house, Dad said, "Okay, everyone, out. Help me with this stuff."

He flipped open the trunk and handed Zayde and Bubbe shopping bags. I got a picnic cooler to carry and Karen lifted a large flat white box. We marched up to the front door, where Dad shifted his bags into one hand and rang the bell.

Uncle Jim opened the door, speaking around the cigar in his mouth. "Well, lookee here!" he exclaimed in his big voice. "You guys don't pack light, do you? Need a hand?" He put his hand out as if to shake Dad's. "Here's one!"

Zayde grumbled. "Har-har. We schlepp, you joke. Grab some of this stuff before I drop it."

We all squeezed past Uncle Jim into the house, but no one was there. Jim pointed down the hall, "They're out back."

Dad ordered me, "Go ahead, Michael. Mrs. G's waiting for that." He nodded at the cooler I carried. "I'll put this other stuff in the kitchen.

I headed out back. All I saw at first were JimmyJoe grinning at me. Then I heard, "Surprise!! Happy Birthday, Michael."

It took me a few seconds to put it together, to see the people in front of me. There were the Giudice kids of course. Coach Fiorello was there with guys from the team. Sam and Sherrie and Uncle Bernie and Aunt Jennie. Eddie Cohen and others from school. Even Nana Minna and Papa Reuben.

There were balloons and a handmade Happy Birthday banner. People started bringing out the boxes and bags from the kitchen. As they emptied them, the pile of wrapped gifts grew.

Dad opened the big white box and took out a huge cake with "Happy 12th Birthday, Michael" in icing. It was decorated with a baseball and bat and a four-fingered mitt!

From another box came a Jell-O dessert, layers of colors with marshmallows and fruit in each. There was a pile of Bubbe's cookies and Mom's Mandelbrot. Not to be outdone, Mrs. G had made her special Norwegian sugar cookies and some of what she called her "American chocolate chips."

"Okay, guys!" Uncle Jim had a Kodak camera hanging from his neck. He motioned us to line up for pictures in big groups in front of the banner, around the cake as I blew out the candles, in groups around the yard. The team with the coaches. The twins with me. My family: Mom, Dad, Karen and me. Then my bigger family with Sam, Sherrie, Uncle Bernie, Aunt Jennie, Bubbe and Zayde and even Mom's parents.

But my favorite picture was the one Jim took of Mom, Dad, Karen, JimmyJoe and Mrs. G. With me in the middle. My big Westside family all smiling at the camera.

CHAPTER TWENTY-THREE

That school year whizzed by. The twins and I were in seventh grade, the youngest kids in a big junior high school that served all the Westside. As I inched down the crowded hall, I would spot one or two of the Columbus Park gang. It was like finding the first letter of your name in a bowl of alphabet soup.

It was in gym class that JimmyJoe and some others from the team wound up together with me. I could have avoided gym because of my back brace. Doc Abrams had written a note explaining the limitations I had but Mr. Jordan, the big tough ex-Marine who was our P.E. teacher, would have none of it. "Friedman," he growled, "I expect you to try your damnedest. If you can't, you can't. Then we will see but now, no excuses."

I took off my brace in the locker room and did all the boring calisthenics and ran all the laps that Mr. Jordan ordered us to do. We went through the sports seasons with touch football which I sucked at, basketball which hurt with the overhead shots and finally, in the spring, softball out in the field.

That was my time to shine. Mr. Jordan marveled at my speed in getting to the ball and my throws to get outs when he thought they were impossible. I was good with a bat, too, getting hits to advance players to score.

His approval meant a lot. He was not family or my Pony League coach or a friend who knew all my struggles. He admired what I could do because I was good.

That year, the twins and I made the varsity team as seventh graders. Perhaps a junior high baseball varsity team doesn't sound like much but, for me, it was a chance to fit in. After being the poor kid, the mediocre student, then Rocky with the smelly body cast, being known as a varsity baseball player let me walk the crowded hallways with pride.

I was also getting ready for my Bar Mitzvah in early October of 1961. That is a big deal in Jewish families, the time a boy gets up in front of the whole congregation to perform blessings and readings in Hebrew to show he has become an adult in our tradition. It takes a lot of work to learn everything. I had Hebrew school three days a week, Tuesday and Thursday afternoons and Sunday mornings.

During baseball season, Dad let me miss some Hebrew classes to go to practice or games. I would make up my absences by studying extra hard with my grandparents and going to shul with Zayde each Saturday morning. Coach Fiorello, being a 'real mensch' as my Zayde said, agreed that I could miss occasional practices to be at Hebrew school. So, all in all, the season went smoothly.

Mom had some relapses of "anxiety." She would get very quiet and spend days in bed. She returned to Chicago State for treatments. Other times her Gaucher's made her very jaundiced, so she had to go to another hospital for transfusions.

If Dad stopped by the ball fields after practice to pick me up, I knew he had just dropped Mom off at one of the hospitals and was heading home, taking a detour to my school. It got to be a routine: when Mom went away, Dad would come by to pick me up.

The good news was I spent a lot more time with Bubbe and Zayde. Karen would go to Aunt Jennie's because she wanted to hang out with Sherrie. She complained that she couldn't stand to listen to me practice my Bar Mitzvah prayers anymore.

As Bubbe had said, she knew the blessings cold. As I helped her make the challah and the dishes for Friday night dinner, we sang the blessings for the Torah and Haftarah readings. I soon knew them by heart.

Each Friday night was a funny, but, I guess, typically American Jewish blend of old and new. We had a traditional Shabbos meal with blessings over the candles, freshly baked challah and wine.

Then we ate Bubbe's Russian Jewish specialties: chicken soup with matzah balls or homemade noodles, beef brisket or roasted chicken, sweet carrot tzimmes, potato kugel and apple cake.

But, after dinner, like the rest of America, Zayde and I watched TV, laughing at Jackie Gleason and Phil Silvers. Bubbe would tsk at us for watching such *umzin* or nonsense on Shabbos but we knew she was peeking at the shows from the kitchen because she laughed at just the right times. Zayde let me stay up late to watch boxing. As we swayed and flinched with the action, we sucked on sour ball candies.

On Saturday morning we walked to the shul just a few blocks from the apartment. "He's never been such a shulgoer," Bubbe whispered to me as I helped clear the breakfast dishes while Zayde got ready. "But, at his age, it is now or never to get in good with the Holy One Blessed Be He. So, you are doing a mitzvah for your Zayde."

On the walk, Zayde said, "I haven't been in shul so much since I had to say the Mourner's Kaddish for my father, blessed is his memory. Now I am there so often they want me on the Board. Tateleh, you are making me into a *gantzer macher*, a big man there. Soon they will ask for more money from me."

Everyone greeted us with a *Gut Shabbos* and a handshake. Zayde announced to each man, "My grandson, Michael. Soon a Bar Mitzvah, God willing. Already a star ballplayer!" I wasn't sure which made him prouder.

I remember those as special times: walking with Zayde, listening to his jokes and stories then sucking on sour balls as we sat side by side for the long service.

In the spring and summer, our Junior Pony team, the Columbus Park Rangers, became the team to beat. We raced up the league standings, easily clinching a spot in the playoffs. Each game, home or away, JimmyJoe and I had our own cheering section. I heard Uncle Jim's trumpet, Dad's yells of anger at the umps and Mrs. G's shouts of encouragement. Mom was there, when she could be. And some cute girls from school hung out in the stands to watch us play.

Even though we lost in the finals, it was a great season. I had become a key player, good for a hit to advance a runner and a great second baseman, robbing our opponents of runs.

The season ended in mid-September, leaving me just two weeks before my Bar Mitzvah. During those weeks, I was scheduled to meet frequently with the cantor to polish my parts of the service and with the rabbi to review my speech.

One afternoon, Dad's big green Belair was waiting at the curb in front of the junior high. I was surprised to find him there. I wondered, *Was Mom back in the hospital? She seemed fine in the morning when we left for school.*

As I got closer, I knew it was very bad news. Dad's face was gray and streaked with tears. "Get in, Michael," he said in a hoarse voice.

When I got in, he turned to me. "My Dad," he rasped out.

It was like being hit by a pitch: I was stunned and couldn't react.

He tried again. "Your Zayde...died this afternoon. Goddamn it! He choked on a goddamn sucker while watching TV. By the time the ambulance got there, it was too late." He heaved a loud sob, then put his head on the steering wheel.

When I touched his arm. he raised his head. "Give me a second, Michael. Okay, I have to pick up Sam, Sherrie and Karen at the high school. I am bringing you all to Mrs. G's house to wait. Jennie and I need to make arrangements. Phone calls. Other stuff." He wiped away his tears then started the car.

Mrs. G opened the door for us then she went to the car where Dad was sitting. They spoke for a few minutes before he drove off.

The Giudices' home was quiet. Sherrie and Karen disappeared upstairs with Connie while Sam and I sat with the twins on the back stoop.

We didn't play Pinners. Instead, they asked us about Zayde. Sam and I talked about his jokes and his arguments with Bubbe and his screams at the TV when he thought the umpires were bums. And his fondness for those stupid sour balls. We laughed even as tears ran down our faces.

When Mrs. G called us in for snack, she had a pad and pencil in front of her. "I need help," she said. "What is appetizing? That is what your dad said Jewish people eat after a funeral. Bagels and appetizing?"

I shrugged and looked at Karen. She answered for us, "Bubbe always serves cream cheese, lox, herring, and whitefish salad with bagels. I guess that is what Dad meant."

"Where would I get those foods?"

"Tiffany's" I blurted.

"On Michigan Avenue?" she asked, surprised.

Karen snorted, "Michael means 'Rosen's' — the store on our street. Because the food there is expensive, everyone calls it Tiffany's."

In the Jewish tradition, funerals happen as soon as possible. Zayde's funeral service was the very next day in the shul we had gone to all those Saturday mornings. It was filled, not only with family, but with members of the congregation. I guess he had really become somewhat of a *macher* there.

When I saw Bubbe, I ran into her arms and broke into sobs. She cried too. "He loved you so much, Michaeleh. He was so proud of you. He wanted to see you a Bar Mitzvah." She sobbed loudly, then added, "I knew in my heart those candies were bad for him. He thought he was such a *chachem*. That he was so smart in the head. *Gut far him.* Good, now he can explain to the Holy One Blessed Be He how he was so smart." She took a deep breath and gave me a hug. "Don't listen to me, tateleh. I am *farklempt*. What will I do now without Abe to yell at?"

My father led Bubbe into the service. I don't remember much but I vividly remember the burial in a cemetery in Forest Park. Dad had said that I was too young to go there but I had yelled back that I was almost a man, just two weeks from my Bar Mitzvah.

Once the coffin was lowered into the ground, each of us took a turn to shovel earth over it. It is an honor to the dead person to have family and friends fill in the grave. I did my share, but I shuddered at each thud of dirt hitting the coffin.

We went back to Bubbe's house for the meal of condolence. Mrs. G greeted us at the door with a pitcher of water and towels to wash our hands, the tradition when you return from a cemetery. She handed round a platter of hard-boiled eggs, another tradition, to symbolize the circle of life. Bubba's dining table was spread with the specialties we had mentioned to Mrs. G.

"Rose, thank you," Dad said. "How did you know all the traditions?"

"Mr. Rosen," she said, "was so helpful, telling me what to do and what to buy."

"I am sure he was," Dad said, eying the laden table. "I am sure he was very happy to help you spend on all this."

Bubbe sat quietly, nodding at friends and family who came to speak with her but saying little. Just muttering, "I warned Abe that those candies would be the death. But he insisted that he had to have small pleasures in life. Now he will miss the big pleasures in life like Michael's Bar Mitzvah."

Dad brought her food. "Mom, eat something. You need to keep your strength up."

She waved a hand at him. "For what do I need strength now?"

"To live, Mom. For me. For your grandkids. For Michael's Bar Mitzvah! For the future."

She shook her head. Dad tightened his lips. "Mom," he said, a sharpness had entered his voice.

"I am angry at Pop, too. Such a stupid way to go, choking on a sour ball, but we must go on."

Bubbe shook her head again. Dad put the plate down on the table next to her then went to greet new visitors.

Mom sat down next to Bubbe and took her hand. "Mom Friedman, I am sad about Abe's death. It was so sudden. But I have good memories of him. He was always kind to me, although it took me a while to understand that since he seemed so gruff. I know that, even when I was not a good wife and mother, he told Dave that it wasn't my fault. He stood up for me. He saved my life by being so kind. I will miss him." Tears began to slide down Mom's face and she grasped Bubbe's hand harder.

Bubbe leaned her head against Mom's and wept with her. "Abe worried about you. He didn't understand all your problems but he kept telling David that he shouldn't blame you for what you couldn't control.

"David is like Abe was when he was young. Impatient and fast to get angry, especially about things he can't control. Like the Depression when we lost the farm in Indiana because we couldn't pay the bank. He hated moving to Chicago but he had to get work wherever he could. Working for others, following orders, not being his own boss nearly killed him.

"But family kept him going on. David and Jennie and me. When the grandkids came, he became a new man, a happier man. Suddenly there was a future again."

I felt hands on my shoulders. I turned to find Mrs. G standing behind me. "Michael, go hug your grandma. You heard her. You're the future."

I went up to Bubbe. As soon as she looked at me, I started crying. "Oh Bubbe" was all I said.

She stood up, wrapped her arms around me and whispered, "Oh, tataleh. It's okay to cry. We are sad because your Zayde is gone. He loved you and was proud of you. Remember, he is always watching out for you." As she wiped my eyes with the Kleenex she had tucked up her sleeve, she added, "Probably still sucking on that *farshiltn* sour ball and kvetching about the Cubs too."

We both chuckled while the tears slid down our cheeks. She picked up the plate Dad had made for her and handed it to me. "Michaeleh, eat. You need strength. You have a big day soon."

CHAPTER TWENTY-FOUR

My Bar Mitzvah was never going to be a "big affair" like Eddie Cohen's was. Saturday night, after the morning service, Eddie's parents held a party in the shul's 'ballroom.' A band played dance music for the adults and there was a game room for the kids. After the roast beef dinner, waiters, in white jackets, wheeled in tables and tables of desserts with another table was set up like a miniature candy store, just for us kids.

We didn't have that kind of money. Dad had warned me that my party would be "modest." Bubbe said it would be *'in gut geshmak,'* in good taste, just a luncheon for family and friends.

I was disappointed. A luncheon would be so lame for my friends after all those big parties. So, Dad had promised to take my friends and me bowling that night after the luncheon.

I now felt differently with Zayde gone. I didn't want anything at all, not a luncheon, not a bowling party. Every time I practiced my chanting, I became sad again at the thought that Zayde was not going to be there, beaming up at me while I said the blessings and chanted my haftarah portion. Most likely, he would have been sucking on a goddamn sour ball as he smiled.

When I met with Rabbi Schwartz the week after Zayde's death, the purpose was to review my speech. Instead, he put aside his copy and said quietly, "Michael, you just had a big loss. Do you want to talk about it?"

Rabbi Schwartz was a young guy with young kids. Since he had grown up in St. Louis, he was a big Cardinals' fan, not an easy thing to be in Chicago. Although it wasn't cool to say so, I liked him a lot. He told goofy jokes and played Pinners with kids on the stoop of the Rabbi's house around the corner from the synagogue.

It wasn't hard to talk to him about Zayde's death. I remember how he started me off. He said, "We feel shock after a sudden death. We are numb. We wonder how life can go on normally for others after our life has changed drastically.

"But, soon, memories begin to warm us up as we recall the happy times, good times, fun times with the departed person. We want to talk about how that person meant so much to us.

"Michael, tell me about your good times with your Zayde."

Once I started, I couldn't stop. Watching Jack Benny and Phil Silvers and boxing. Walking to shul with him. Sneaking out to Montrose Beach to buy snacks to eat on a bench as we talked about baseball. His funny arguments with Bubbe. And even both of us sucking on those big sour balls which he loved so much but which killed him in that freakish way.

Rabbi Schwartz rocked back in his chair, smiling and laughing at the right spots. Then he said thoughtfully, "I've read your D'var Torah where you connect the Torah portion to your life. Your portion describes Abraham's life from when he is commanded to leave his homeland to journey far and wide. God promises to build a nation from his descendants, but Abraham wonders how that could happen. After all, he had no son with his wife Sarah. When he is a hundred years old and Sarah is ninety, a miracle happens: they have a son, Isaac, who will live out God's promise. The whole story is about the future of a family.

"Your Zayde's name was Abraham. Perhaps that is a good starting place for you, Michael. Talk about the first Abraham, the Biblical one, then about your grandfather Abraham, his life's story and his importance to you and your family. That would be a great D'var Torah for everyone to hear: how the people in our lives leave us so much richer for having been with us.

"Let your Dad help you by telling you his memories of his father. That would be a blessing to both of you. You lost your Zayde but he lost his father."

That's what I did. Dad was sitting shiva in Bubbe's apartment for seven days after the funeral. He arrived there after his shift at Veriflex. He said the Veriflex people wouldn't understand Jewish traditions. Greenbaum did, of course, so Dad didn't have to go to his second job that week.

He drove me with him to Bubbe's each day after school. As he sat on the low chair designated for mourners, we talked. I heard stories about the farm and Indiana. I learned that Zayde had showed up at each baseball home game to cheer loudly for my Dad and to yell back at anyone who called Dad a 'dirty Jew' or "a kike."

While Bubbe was out of the room, Dad whispered that Zayde got into fights when he had enough of the name-calling. "He told your Bubbe that his bruises were from falling down the bleachers."

"I knew," Bubbe yelled from the kitchen. "Falling?! Hah! It was too much acting like a big tough guy." She came into the living room wiping her hands on a dish towel as she added, "He never could ignore dreck from the mouth of a *nisht gutnick*, a no-goodnik. He wanted the world to be a better place for the *kinder*, the children. He should only have gotten his wish."

Bubbe then brought us a stack of scrapbooks. As she laid them down on the coffee table, Dad said, "I haven't seen these for years. I wondered what had happened to them."

Bubbe replied, "No matter where we moved or how little space we had, these came with us. Abe always packed them carefully. They were precious to him. Now you must keep them safe."

Old cord ran through the holes that held the pages together and the tape that kept the clippings in place was yellowed and cracked with age. They were filled with newspaper reports of Dad's baseball career, his name underlined in each story, his face circled in each picture. Dad wiped his eyes with a Kleenex as he slowly turned the pages.

The last book, however, was different from the rest. It was brand new with a dark-green cover and shiny brass brads. Dad handed it to me. There, on the first page, was a single photo. Me in my first baseball uniform.

"Your Zayde started this when you first made the team," Dad said.

He turned to the page of the newspaper write-up of the playoff game we lost to the Bronzeville team. My name was underlined each place it appeared. M. Friedman, second base. M. Friedman picking off a runner. M. Friedman stealing second.

Dad said, "I'll keep up this Friedman tradition and add to this book, Michael. As my Dad did for me, I will do for you."

I wasn't nervous by the day of my Bar Mitzvah. Everyone else's nervousness had worn away my own and left me numb.

Dad had picked Bubbe up early because she insisted on cooking breakfast for us. "It's not good to start an important day with an empty stomach," she said.

She kept telling us to eat so our stomachs wouldn't rumble during the service. I tried but I couldn't get much down as chaos swirled around me. Her bustling and urging gave me the jitters.

It got worse when Karen complained about her dress, her hair, her makeup. Mom couldn't remember where she had put her hat, her gloves, her purse. Dad kept asking: Did I have my new Tallit, my Kippah, my speech? Yes, yes, yes. Did I want to go over the chanting again, read the speech again? No and no.

I decided to wait on the front stoop. I sat down carefully, using the pages of my speech to keep the seat of my new suit clean. I was surprised to see the twins, all dressed up in new suits, walking towards me.

They, of course, along with Mrs. G and Connie and Uncle Jim, had been invited to my Bar Mitzvah but JimmyJoe were headed in the wrong direction.

Towards me, instead of towards the synagogue in Uncle Jim's station wagon.

Joey announced as they reached me. "Mom wanted us out of the house because we were making her nervous. Connie was doing stuff to her hair and all. I guess it wasn't coming out so good."

I spread out more pages of my speech so the twins could sit and keep their suits clean too.

"Nervous?" Jimmy asked me.

"Not anymore. I want to get it over with."

"Well, don't worry," Joey added. "We'll be there, cheering you on. Uncle Jim is bringing his trumpet to blow, like he did at our games." His smile revealed it was a joke.

"Too bad your grandpa won't be there," Jimmy said. "He was a great guy."

I said, "He'll be there...at least in spirit. The whole family all together. That's what I will talk about." I pointed to the papers under us. "About families. The families we are born into and the families we find when people care about us."

"Like us," JimmyJoe said together.

Just then, the door to the house opened and Dad marched out, followed by Bubbe, Mom and Karen. "Okay, Michael," he said. "Pile into the car. We need to get to the synagogue early."

The twins stood up and helped me collect the pages of my speech. They hesitated then took a step back in the direction of the parking lot by The Church.

"Wait," Dad called out to them. "It'll be a real squeeze but, boys, get in the back seat."

So the triplets, JimmyJoe Michael, piled in, mashed up close together. We had our arms around each other's shoulders and our heads touching.

Dad's Belair slowly took off down the block, past the parking lot between The Church and the synagogue we didn't go to anymore. Past the parking lot that led to Gladys Street where so many of the new blessings in my life had begun.

AFTERWORD

We hope you enjoyed this novel based on a combination of our family stories. Events have been created or streamlined and characters and conversations added to bolster the main themes. We wanted to give readers a "true" sense of a child who, while challenged by physical problems as well as the mental, physical and emotional issues that plagued his family, found caring adults to provide him with loving support.

As indie authors, we depend on the reviews of readers to spread the word about our work. We would be grateful if you took a moment to post a review on Amazon.com or Goodreads.com or anywhere else avid readers congregate. We are available to give talks to organizations, book clubs or libraries, either in person, or using Facetime or Skype. Contact us at WLM.and.MLW@gmail.com. We can also customize guides for book groups as well.

Several diseases are described in the novel. For more information, these websites are good places to start:

Gaucher's Disease:

https://www.genome.gov/25521505/learning-about-gaucher-disease/

Scheuermann's Disease:

https://www.spine-health.com/conditions/
spinal-deformities/scheuermanns-disease-
thoracic-and-lumbar-spine

Depression suffered by women:
https://www.nimh.nih.gov/health/publications/de
pression-in-women/index.shtml#pub1

For a historic view of anxiety in women and its treatment, the authors referred to:

Horwitz, A. V. (2010). How an Age of Anxiety Became an Age of Depression. *The Milbank Quarterly, 88*(1), 112–138. http://doi.org/10.1111/j.1468-0009.2010.00591.x

Payne, N. A., & Prudic, J. (2009). Electroconvulsive Therapy Part I: A Perspective on the Evolution and Current Practice of ECT. *Journal of Psychiatric Practice, 15*(5), 346–368. http://doi.org/10.1097/01.pra.0000361277.65468.ef

About the Authors

<u>Wayne L. Meyer's</u> childhood on Chicago's Westside inspired Michael's story. Like Michael, Wayne's childhood was darkened by his mother's illnesses, his own ailments, his father's financial struggles, and the family's secrets. But after a run-in with twin brothers, Wayne's life was changed by the twins' friendship and their mother's love. As a shared passion for baseball drew him closer to his father, Wayne went on to an athletic career that included letters in high school varsity baseball and wrestling. The twins were always his team-mates. In their sophomore year, their high school varsity baseball team won the Chicago City Championship at Wrigley Field. After college, Wayne played for the semi-pro Chicago Stars and was scouted by the St. Louis Cardinals.

Happily married for 44 years (the twins were his best men at the wedding), Wayne is the proud father of two adult children and "Zayde" to four grandchildren. He still lives in the Chicago region and still roots for the Cubs. His dad lived to see the Cubs win the 2016 World Series win, a lifelong dream come true. Wayne still hangs out with the twins several times a year.

<u>Meryl L. Wilens</u> was born in The Bronx, NY, but grew up on Long Island. Despite the move to the "country," away from her grandparents, they remained important in her life. She was a rapt

listener to all their "kibitzing" over cards and "glasses" of tea. Now retired from a career in academia, she has been busy preserving their tales through fiction.

Career moves took Meryl and her husband to the Chicago area. There she met Wayne and his wife. One day, he began to tell her the stories of his childhood and showed her all the scrapbooks.

"That would make a great book," Meryl said, "but I write fiction. Are you okay with that?"

Wayne agreed and their partnership was launched.

Meryl's next book will be based on her mother's tales of the women in their Long Island neighborhood in the fifties. Now she and her husband are back in NY, enjoying being Bubbe and Zayde to two wonderful grandchildren (with hopes of more to come). They are also parents to two adult children and their partners from whom they *shepp nachas*, get great joy!